So You Wanna Be a Cowgirl

Patricia Probert Gott

Best Wishes,
Pat Gott aug '07

PublishAmerica
Baltimore

First printing

At the specific preference of the author, PublishAmerica allowed this work to remain exactly as the author intended, verbatim, without editorial input.

Rimrock is a real dude ranch and was owned and operated by Glenn and Alice Fales. However, all other characters' names were changed to protect their privacy.

Cover Picture: Author is astride her guide horse Navaho atop Table Mountain, Shoshone National Forest, Park County, Wyoming. The young girl is the author's granddaughter.

Front Cover designed by Patricia Gott and illustrated by Laura Wiley Ashton www.gitflorida.com.

ISBN: 1-4241-7569-0
PUBLISHED BY PUBLISHAMERICA, LLLP
www.publishamerica.com
Baltimore

Printed in the United States of America

DEDICATION

To Glenn Fales, posthumously, an old cowboy
with a big heart and a lack of prejudice that enabled
an aging lady from the East, with an Arabian horse,
to experience the adventures of being a cowgirl in the
West. I will be forever grateful.

PROLOGUE

Many young girls dream of horses. Some take lessons and learn to ride; the rest of us live and breathe all aspects of horses—drawing, painting, scrap booking, playing horse games, and forever scheming to own one. Any horse will do, just so we can brush, braid, hug, and ride. We read *The Black Stallion* series with fervor. We imagine being a cowgirl riding the backcountry of Wyoming, after reading *My Friend Flicka* or *Thunderhead*. Some take it a little farther than dreaming, as I did.

During the summer of my eighth year, my dad bought a farm outside of town and I got an old Shetland pony. All I had to do was promise to stop biting my fingernails, and to be responsible for the pony's barn chores and taking care of him. No problem—I was in seventh heaven.

From that old pony, I progressed through my senior year in high school free-leasing or buying horses. First was a retired draft horse, then a sway-backed old Thoroughbred mare, a Welch pony, a Morgan horse and lastly, a two-year-old pinto Quarter-horse gelding which I trained into a fine western trail horse.

As most kids do when left to their own ingenuity around horses, we taught our horses to rear, like Lone Ranger's horse, Silver; sometimes staying on, sometimes falling off. We vaulted over their rumps onto their backs Roy Rogers's style, and raced each other to see who had the fastest horse that day. When we weren't racing, we were playing "Cowgirls and Indians". Because I rode bareback, I often played an Indian, even riding with a war bridle—a loop around the horse's jaw. When playing a cowgirl, I taught all my steeds to halt whenever I threw the reins and to ground-tie like good cowponies.

This wasn't exactly my idea of being a cowgirl but it would do until the real thing came along.

Many years (and many horses) later, the real thing did come along. I had the chance to work summers at a dude ranch outside Cody, Wyoming as a ranch wrangler and guide.

I was going be a real cowgirl…this is my story.

CHAPTER 1

With my car window rolled down I stared in awe out at my surroundings in the Wapiti Valley. The air rushing in was much cooler than I had expected. After all, I remembered, it's still May, and I'd been warned that in this part of Wyoming it was apt to be chilly with possible cold rains or snow through mid-June. I pulled off the road and got out of my car to get a better view. It had been a long four-day drive from my home in Maine to Cody, Wyoming; but this scene, perfect as a postcard, showed that this trip was going to be well worth it.

On my left a large herd of horses grazed peacefully on irrigated pasture grass alongside the highway, while in the background, sagebrush and prickly-pear cacti sunbathed on the arid soil of rolling hills. Snow-capped mountains formed the northern horizon to my right, I later learned it was the Absaroka Range of the Rocky Mountains. The Shoshone River, lined with pine and cottonwood trees, wound west/east through the valley and puffy white clouds, so near you could almost reach up and touch them, dotted the brilliant blue sky overhead. The clarity of the air helped make the view spectacular.

The scenery was even more resplendent than I'd ever dared dream when Glenn Fales had said that my horse and I were hired to work at Rimrock Dude Ranch for the summer. I was a 40-year-old divorced businesswoman from Maine going to work as a ranch wrangler and my 7-year-old Arabian gelding would be one of my guide horses.

Razan, my horse, traveled via commercial horse carrier from Maine to Rimrock Ranch. I called Alice Fales, Glenn's wife, when I arrived in Cody, asking for driving directions to Rimrock and she told me my horse had arrived safely a couple of days ago, thankfully. He was being isolated in a small corral getting acquainted through the fence with the other 125 ranch horses and pack mules. I had worried about Razan's well being while he was travelling in the care of others. Would he drink enough to keep hydrated, or load and unload without problems at stopovers? I had raised Razan from a yearling, training him myself, and as other horse owners/horse lovers tended to do, treated him like a family member.

Looking ahead, I could see what I supposed was "The Rim" jutting out nearly a mile long and rising 500 feet above a ranch I assumed was Rimrock. The ranch was located 26 miles west of Cody on the North Fork Highway leading to Yellowstone. Teddy Roosevelt once said that this drive following the North Fork of the Shoshone River from Cody to Yellowstone Park was "The most scenic 52 miles in America." I could not agree with him more.

With eager anticipation, I got back into my car and drove on toward The Rim. It was time I introduced myself to Glenn, Alice, and my fellow wranglers. I had met Glenn and Alice briefly four years ago when I'd been a guest on a horse pack trip going from Cody to Jackson Hole with Rimrock as the outfitter. The Fales had hosted a pre-departure dinner for six other guest-riders and myself the night before we were to begin our 10-day, 100-mile adventure, riding over the Rocky Mountains. Alice told us we'd never forget it—how right she was!

I knew a little about the couple from pack-trip campfire chatter and telephone conversations with Glenn over the past winter. Glenn and Alice, now in their 70's, had owned Rimrock Ranch for 35 years. Glenn had been a rodeo bronc rider in his younger days and now, years later, suffered the consequences of being thrown to the ground time after time by bucking horses. Although he was a little stiff and arthritic, he still rode his horse, Ronnie, with his friends when they came to the ranch as guests. His horse was named after President Ronald Reagan who'd been a guest at Rimrock Ranch in the 80's. Glenn's domain was anything to do with the horses, corrals, wranglers, day rides, and pack trips. His priority was pleasing his guests in any way possible and many returned year after year because of his accommodating ways. He ran his ranch hands-on style according to his employees; his word was law. They called him "Chief" out of respect.

Alice oversaw the bookkeeping, cleaning, cooking, waitress, and yard staff; handled reservations, ordered supplies, and scheduled outside ranch activities, i.e. weekly rafting trips down the Shoshone, day trips to Yellowstone Park. Yet, she somehow managed to find time to ride her Arabian horse, Casper, occasionally. She was well respected by employees and guests alike.

CHAPTER 2

Rimrock Ranch's driveway was a mile long. I drove over the proverbial slatted western cattle/horse guard that ensured animals did not go beyond that point. Westerners honored a "fence-out" law, while Easterners, a "fence-in" law. I passed Glenn and Alice's home on the left, setback from the ranch road for privacy. A little further on there were two small pastures. A couple of horses that appeared to have medical problems were grazing in one and the other pasture had some young horses, maybe yearlings, in it.

Then came the ranch pond that I later learned was amply stocked with trout for guests to catch and throw back. The large rodeo arena was vacant but the stock corrals were full of horses —and there was Razan, I noticed, looking not-so-content in his small adjacent corral. What stood out right away was that most of the horses were chestnuts or bays, with very few pintos or appaloosas. I knew that brown horses tended to accept other brown horses fairly easily and was pretty sure that Razan, being a chestnut and also a non-aggressive type, would readily acquiesce and fit in. He'd be content at the bottom of the pecking order as long as he was with the other horses. I would integrate him with the rest as soon as I had a chance to consult with Glenn.

As I drove straight ahead to the main ranch house, I could see the snow-topped peak of Ptarmigan Mountain in the background, framed between Green Creek Ridge and The Rim. What a magnificent picture! I took several shots with my new camera. The ranch house was a log-style lodge, surrounded by an open porch. I noticed a stone chimney protruding from the roof and along the backside, hoping it might be for a huge, homey fireplace. The lodge looked large enough to contain the dining area and kitchen also.

I had a fleeting moment of uncertainty about my drastic decision to come 2500 miles west to work, especially bringing my own horse with me and exposing him to all kind of unknown conditions, i.e. weather, feed, and terrain. The ranch was already at a mile high elevation where simply breathing was going to take getting used to. Oh well, Glenn hadn't discouraged me; I was already here; it was too late to back out now.

Putting my sudden anxiety aside, I parked my red Chevy Beretta, now more than a few miles past any good trade-in value, in the guests' parking lot. I took my time looking around before entering the lodge. There were nine rustic-looking log cabins, for guests apparently. Glenn had said that the ranch could accommodate 46 guests at peak season. What looked like a feed shed and another large building were tucked behind and under some cottonwood trees. I correctly supposed all the tack, saddles, and horse supplies were stored in this larger building because several hitching rails were adjacent to it. Also next to the parking area was a long open shed, maybe for maintenance and for the repairmen to use. I wondered where the employees quarters were and what my accommodations would be like.

No time like the present to find out.

I walked up the porch steps and knocked on the door. A good-looking, and noticeably, long-legged cowboy answered the door. I gulped, stared at his gorgeous dark eyes, twinkling under his Stetson's brim, and thought simply: "Wow!"

"Hi, I'm Pat Gott," I managed to say. "I'm going to be working here this summer and I'm supposed to meet either Glenn or Alice Fales. They're expecting me."

"Howdy ma'am, I'm Dustin," the cowboy smiled and replied. "I used to work for Glenn but I run my own outfit these days up near Pahaska packing into Yellowstone. I just stopped by to say 'Hi' on my way into town.

"Glenn's gone with a couple of the boys checking trails, but Alice is down back in one of the cabins. I just talked to her so she should be along soon. I was on my way out, but you can wait in here if you want."

"I'd like to get unpacked but I don't know where to park my car or myself. I guess I could wander around until I find Alice."

"Yes, but first, why don't you pull your car around back; that's where the help always parks. I'd offer to help you carry your stuff but I don't know which bunkhouse you'll be in."

"That's okay, thanks for the offer and nice meeting you. Maybe I'll see you around this summer."

"Same here, ma'am."

Hmmmm, that was interesting. Things were looking good, literally.

I drove my car around back like Dustin had said and found a parking spot not far from the bunkhouses. There were three single-story buildings, each about the size of a house trailer, and two smaller ones. I found and pocketed the map of Rimrock's ranch and land that Glenn had sent me, put on my hiking boots, and set off to explore, find Alice, and check on Razan—not necessarily in that order.

CHAPTER 3

On my way to the corrals, I spotted a building called The Store. No one was there, but there was a lot of merchandise, i.e. souvenir type goods of woven Indian rugs, postcards, key chains and western accessories of every kind, limited only by sizes and quantity. There were socks, T-shirts, gloves, caps, rain ponchos, belts, and bandanas, along with necessities like bandaids, aspirin, and tampons. I wondered, who are these items for, are they ranch supplies, or merchandise for sale, and how would I purchase something? I figured, I'll just add these to my many other questions for Glenn or Alice, when I finally meet them.

I nosed around down by the hitching rails and found a wranglers' saddle shed and horse shoeing area. It looked like they'd been busy picking tails and clipping bridle paths as horse hair was abundant on the ground – as were several piles of recent manure. A keg of new horseshoes of various sizes and shoeing nails were just inside the feed room door. I noticed that all the shoes were "cocked", must be so they won't slip climbing up and down these rugged mountains, I thought.

Down to the corral, Razan whinnied when he saw me. "Good boy," I said as I patted his sleek neck. "How are you?

You look pretty good." But he wasn't happy. He fretted nervously back and forth wanting to join the other horses. I looked around to make sure he had water. Guess so—his drinking source was Canyon Creek that ran through Rimrock's 1500 acres, furnishing water not only for the horses but also for irrigating nearby pasturelands. I could also see he'd been given plenty of alfalfa hay but wasn't eating much of it.

Just then, I heard a truck pull up the drive and stop. A couple of cowboys got out along with an older man I figured was Glenn. Finally, I thought, I'll get some answers and get us settled in. Glenn waved to me and shuffled stiffly to the corrals. He wore cowboy boots, jeans, long-sleeved shirt with sheepskin vest, cowboy hat, and a smile. Glenn had a twinkle in his eye. Throughout the summer, he would kid me about my *Arab* horse, "Raisin", as Glenn called him, and my use of western language—or lack of it. "The Wyoming word for field is meadow," he'd say, "it's a creek not a brook, and you tie your horse not hitch him."

"Howdy, guess you're Pat."

"Right, and you're Glenn, pleased to meet you." He had a real firm handshake.

"So what are we going to do with that *Arab* of yours? He's not eating much but he looks okay and he's not colicky."

"I'd like to put him in with the others if that's okay with you."

"We can try it. We were waiting until you got here to see what you wanted to do with him. Go open his gate and we'll see how he adjusts."

Thus Razan was set free from his enclosure and joined the Rimrock horse herd. There were a few squeals, tail swishes, threats to kick, and necks snaking out to bite, but within a few minutes all had quieted down. Razan kept his attention on the most dominant horses, particularly difficult when he was eating hay from the bins with his rear to the herd. After receiving a few nips and bites over the next few days, he learned to wait until most of the others had their fill, then go to a hay bin that wasn't crowded.

****

Glenn said he and Alice had decided that because of my different job and work hours, I would bunk separately from the other female help. Being a loner, this was just fine with me. A young man named Fred, not exactly the rugged, masculine type like I imagined most ranch hands to be, but nice, came from the kitchen and helped me unload and carry my suitcases and gear to my small cabin. He said he was a pack-trip cook but helped Marla, the ranch cook, until the mountain trips started in July. Fred told me that lunch was at noon; he or Marla would clang a bell when it was time to eat—and "Do not be late." Food was plentiful but hungry help and guests did not wait for anyone.

I took in my surroundings. Opposite my cabin porch was the men's shower and toilet facility; I was not too impressed with that sight. My room was about 12-foot square and held a full size bed, chest of draws, lots of wall hooks, and a separate nook containing a toilet and wash sink. I wondered where I bathed or showered. I sure hoped I didn't have to share the men's showers—now that's something to think about. I unpacked, putting my waterproof and insulated LLBean boots and my cowboy boots by the door. I hung my jeans, jacket, and rain slicker on the wall hooks, and put my shirts, socks, and undies inside the chest of drawers. There was room for my coffeepot on top. Besides my toiletries, I kept the rest of my belongings in my suitcase, which I slid under the bed. Curtains covered a small window over the bed and a picture window looked out across Canyon Creek and the log cabins beyond. All-in-all, the cabin was sufficient and I was making it my home. I could live here comfortably for however long.

CHAPTER 4

Fred was right; the lunch bell rang promptly at noon—right outside my cabin. On my way to the dining room, I met two more employees, a cabin girl named Ann and waitress named Debby. Ann, a sweet girl from Virginia, had just graduated from an equestrienne college. Debby was a friendly transient also interested in horsemanship. Their quarters were in the ladies bunkhouse across the yard from me. They told me I could use their shower facility. It would be especially convenient before dinners, as all the ladies worked during that time.

The dining room was larger than it looked from the outside, containing six round tables and two long rectangle tables that would sit 10-12 people. A luncheon buffet of cold meats, an assortment of cheeses, a couple of cold salads, cold drinks, and cookies and/or chocolate pudding for dessert, was set up in the center.

I was hungry. I filled my plate and sat at the first round table for eight that I came to. Sitting at the table already were Glenn and the two other cowboys I had seen with him in the truck. Actually, I quickly learned they were wranglers not cowboys. Cowboys dealt with cows, wranglers with horses.

Glenn introduced me to Tom Borman, who was the head wrangler, and to Rand Stratan, a fellow ranch wrangler like myself. Rand was a good-looking young man with a beautiful smile. He attended Montana State College and had worked for Glenn in past summers, last year as the head wrangler. Glenn treated him as his son; I liked him immediately. We struck up a good mother/son relationship over the summer. Rand came to me for personal advice. He was only 18- years old and was like my own son. He'd thoughtfully lift the heavier saddles onto the taller horses for me, if he saw I was struggling.

Tom was older and my first impression was that he either did not like me personally or did not like me working for him as a wrangler. Maybe he was just unhappy with his job. Glenn asked him to saddle Phyllis, the ranch's college trained buckskin mare, and take "Raisin" and I out on the trails in the afternoon and show us the ranch land.

"Meet me at the corrals at one o'clock," Tom growled and got up from the table.

"Do you need a saddle and bridle?" Glenn asked.

"No thanks, I brought my own. It's in the trunk of my car but I'll get it down to the saddling area.

"See you at one, Tom."

Glenn told me that there were three more wranglers coming to work tomorrow, Sunday, as well as seven guests for the week. He explained that most guests booked reservations mid-June through the last of August when schools are closed.

"We always have a guest orientation Sunday evenings after our outdoor cookout," Glenn said, "which should answer many of your questions. And I've scheduled a wrangler meeting after breakfast on Monday at the wranglers' shed.

"Tom should be able to familiarize you with the ranch on your ride this afternoon."

Dressed in my favorite Akubra Australian hat, long-sleeved shirt, denim vest, wrangler jeans, cowgirl boots, and leather riding gloves, I saddled my horse, donned my chaps and was ready to ride. I'd acquired my western gear over the past five years doing pack trips in Wyoming, Arizona, and Colorado. The chaps were new.

Razan and I followed Tom and Phyllis past the feed shed to a trail that immediately crossed the East Fork of Canyon Creek, and then climbed switchbacks up, and up, and up. Razan was doing a little puffing, I was trying not to look back and/or down, and Tom was silently riding ahead astride Phyllis. Was this some kind of endurance test for my horse and/or a test of my own fortitude, I wondered.

We rode for another fifteen minutes toward some high cliffs over the flat top of the bluff we'd just climbed. The trail turned south and we rode nearly a half-mile along the base of the cliffs where golden eagles frequently nested. I wanted to know more about the land and if Tom wasn't going to volunteer information, I'd just have to ask.

"Are we still on Glenn's land?" I asked.

"Yep," was all Tom offered.

"How many acres of horse pasture does he own?" I tried again.

"About 600," Tom reply.

"Is that all? Looks like more."

"Most of what you see west and south is The Shoshone National Forest separated by the East and West Forks of Canyon Creek. We'll turn back and head a mile or so east to Green Creek. At the creek, Rimrock's land runs into the Washakie National Forest. With the National Forests bordering three sides of Glenn's land he doesn't have to own much trail land."

"Do the horses have free run of all this land for pasture?"

"No, the horses graze this land close to the ranch only when it's still green in the spring. Glenn leases the irrigated pastures along both sides of the main highway during the dry summers."

"How do you find all the horses out here?" I asked.

Tom turned around and said with a smirk, "That's what you're here for. You wranglers round up the horses every morning. They stay in the corrals or are ridden during the day, then you drive them back to a pasture every evening."

Okay, that might have been more information than I needed right now. I'd have to think about that for a while.

We rode quietly east toward Green Creek, Razan following Phyllis up and down steep slopes and across a flooded high meadow. At times, the trail ascended so steeply that I had to reach forward and hold onto Razan's mane. I leaned back in the saddle a little and pressed my stirrups forward to help my horse balance going down steep narrow inclines. I found myself sometimes holding my breath but Razan seemed to be doing fine.

Back at the corrals a couple hours later, Tom said, "That was your introductory ride. You're on your own from now on."

CHAPTER 5

The next day being Sunday, no one worked in the morning so I knew my services wouldn't be required. I saddled my horse and set out on my own to explore the ranch trails. I figured there were enough points of reference to keep my directional bearings in tact, i.e. The Rim to the west, Ptarmigan Mt to the south, and the Eagle Cliffs to the east.

I started following a trail I had seen behind the bunkhouses. It too crossed Canyon Creek then ascended slightly through aspens and cottonwoods that grew along the creek. Out in the open the land was sage and grass prairie and was easy to cover at a nice trot. Razan was a little apprehensive without Phyllis to follow, especially when we came to where the trail dipped down a side-slope, with a fifty-foot drop-off to the right. A stream of water running across the trail had washed out some of the trail making it difficult for my horse to maintain his footing.

Rounding a corner and coming out of a group of cedars, I saw a moose drinking from a small pond off to my left. Coming from Maine I was familiar with moose and knew by its size that it was no more than a yearling. However, I didn't know how long young moose stayed with its mother and didn't want to hang around to see if the cow was nearby. I trotted off through an open area of mainly sagebrush before the trail disappeared into a group of evergreens. This trail, with the Eagle Cliffs on my right, must be the same trail that Tom and I were riding yesterday before we traversed to Green Creek. Recognizing my surroundings increased my confidence.

Content with the quiet of the forest's tranquility, I didn't see two mule deer partially hidden in a shelter of spruce trees. They startled my horse, suddenly leaping across the trail ahead of me and continuing through the conifers. I noticed the forests were different here in the west. Unlike Maine, there was no thick underbrush to contend with so I could go off-trail without difficulty, which I did.

I reined Razan left to where the deer had come from and discovered a fair-sized secluded pond, seemingly spring-fed as I couldn't see any inlet. From the pond, I had a clear view across to The Rim and spotted a bighorn sheep near the top of a steep trail—maybe a horse trail, as there were indications of switchbacks. What a nice spot! I wondered if we could swim here when it gets warmer. If someone cleaned the pond and dammed the outlet, it would make a natural swimming pool, I thought. Later, when I approached Glenn with the idea, I learned that water is so scarce in Wyoming that it is unlawful to vary a natural water supply, no matter how trivial it may seem. So much for that idea.

We ascended another very steep slope climbing upward toward the peak. Before reaching the apex, I saw a pair of golden eagles landing in the cliffs above. I figured they were making a nest there as I'd been told the cliffs were called Eagle Cliffs.

After exploring for an hour, I dismounted to give my horse a break and I could take some pictures at the same time. I chuckled to myself because Razan was looking around at the spectacular scenery as if he was a tourist himself. "Guess we'd better gaze to our hearts content now, ol' friend," I said, "and not when we're guiding guests on trail rides."

I looked north toward Jim Mountain; snow still blanketed its high meadows as it hovered protectively over the Shoshone and Wapiti Valley. The panoramic view was breathtaking. I could see east as far as the Buffalo Bill Reservoir area fifteen miles away. The multi-million dollar, 353-foot dam housed a huge reservoir of irrigation water for farmers in the lowlands and was popular for fishing and boating.

During the last half of the loop back to the ranch, the trail wound down over slopes and beside dry ravines. It was arid land with only sagebrush and prairie grass growing. Jackrabbits were everywhere and, needless-to-say, so were red tailed hawks and coyotes whose main menu was rabbit. I spotted a coyote entering a den in the side of a ravine. This would be a good guest topic later in the summer when the pups emerged.

I made it back to the ranch just in time for lunch. Three more wranglers had arrived and were waiting in the chow line. Sean Braggon, Travis Barga, and Cole Freely, all from the Cody-Powell, Wyoming area, were college friends of Rand's. They were all nice-looking young men, dressed in colorful western shirts, jeans and cowboy boots. I learned that Glenn required his help to wear western attire while at the ranch at all times. I wondered where their Stetson's were, then saw them all hung on antler hat racks above the archway, including Glenn's. Alice did not allow hats at the dining tables.

All three shook my hand, appearing gracious and pleased to meet me. Sean and Cole were first-time wranglers at Rimrock the same as I. Sean brought a smile, and could sing and play guitar. His idol was country music singer Chris LeDoux and he looked like Garth Brooks. Cole brought his boyish charm and sense of humor. Tall, lean Travis, who had worked at Rimrock last year, was a flirt. I liked them all.

The guests arrived during the afternoon and Tom fitted them to saddles. There were two families: one, a middle age couple with an adult daughter, the other, two sisters and their husbands. I waited until the evening outdoor cookout to mingle.

At the guest orientation, I joined the other employees singing *The Rimrock Song* to the tune of *My Heroes Have Always Been Cowboys*, accompanied by Fred and Sean playing their guitars. Introductions were made all the way around and Glenn assigned horses according to the guests' riding abilities. He gave a brief outline of the coming week's activities and told the guests Rimrock assumed they would participate unless they signed out at least four hours in advance.

I learned that The Store was for the convenience of employees and guests, with no attendant. It operated on the honor system. Purchases were brought to the lodge's front desk for payment. There was no TV on the property and only one telephone, a pay phone outside the kitchen door.

Glenn said for guests to gather at the corrals no later than nine o'clock tomorrow morning to meet their horses and prepare for their introductory ride.

CHAPTER 6

I awoke to a dreary, misty, cold morning. After a hearty breakfast of buckwheat pancakes and lean bacon, orange juice and coffee, all wranglers met with Glenn, "Chief," at the wranglers' shed.

I had looked forward to the meeting and learning what a wrangler's (my) responsibilities were. I had thought about bringing a clipboard to take notes but didn't think that would look too cool. I planned to hurry back to my cabin to write it all down after the meeting, though.

Just as the meeting started, it began to rain so all seven of us moved into the small shed—close quarters.

Chief began by assigning a horse to each wrangler for the summer. Mine was a small but very lively pinto named Navaho. He could (and would) move instantly, whether chasing a straying horse back into the herd or climbing a riverbank to rescue a guest in trouble. No question, Navaho was quick.

Rand was happy to have King, a seasoned alpha male chestnut gelding, with an attitude. Cole was assigned Cody, a swift blue-roan gelding. Travis would ride an airhead chestnut named Deuce. Sean was assigned another alpha male sorrel,

Penny; and Tom kept Adobe, a big-boned, dark-gray mustang he'd been riding. Other horses we could use to wrangle were Fiddler, Nemo, Ace, Patrick, Taxi and Reno. However, Glenn said that *every* horse was to be ridden at least once, to get their winter kinks out and checked for soundness before they were assigned to guests.

The most important tasks at hand over the next two weeks would be, not only to ride each horse, but ensure every horse was shoed, wormed, checked for scratches or sores, bridle path clipped, and tails groomed and picked. That was quite an undertaking as Rimrock had 14 pack mules, 6 draft/pack horses, 100 riding horses, and 5 young mustangs.

On top of that, fences needed to be checked and mended, trails cleared, and irrigation ditches dug. Thankfully, two more wranglers would be arriving during the week. There was plenty of work for all.

Tom spoke up and said that he'd like to go over what he expected from the wranglers. Chief said, "I still run the ranch so I'll tell them what I expect and you can make sure it's carried out."

Ouch, I thought. That won't help Tom's disposition any.

Glenn said that he liked the boys to maintain a clean-cut cowboy image by not swearing, using foul language, or being rude. "And, please train or discipline horses in *private*, not in front of the guests."

In addition, he said, "When you bring the horses in from the pasture, a steady trot will keep them moving together and get them here in good condition.

"Remember that guests are most important and it's good for you to mingle and get to know them."

"Any questions?"

"How do we know when we are supposed to wrangle? And what time do we begin?" Cole asked.

"Next week, after all wranglers have reported to work, Tom will assign wrangle partners for the summer. Until then, check with him every evening. The wranglers assigned for that day arrive at the corrals by 6:15 am. Horses are taken back out to pasture when we're all through with them, usually about 4:30-5:00 pm," Glenn replied.

"Oh, and whenever possible, I'd like you to rope the horses when you catch them in the round pen. Guests love to see cowboys use their lariat," Glenn added.

Well that leaves me out, I thought. I wonder if I can learn to rope a horse in one easy lesson!

"Rand, anything else to add?"

"Just that as in the past, wranglers are responsible for keeping tack cleaned and repaired. And I don't know if most of you do this or not, but Rimrock uses double blankets and breast collars on all horses. While you're saddling up, make sure the bridle and saddle fit. Last year we had some problems with saddles slipping because narrow-tree saddles were put onto round-backed horses. And wide trees on high-withered horses won't work either. So pay attention while you saddle up and tell Tom if there's a problem with the fit."

Chief agreed.

The rain was pouring down when the meeting broke up at 8:30. Glenn went to the lodge to see if or how many guests still wanted to ride. Meanwhile I scooted back to my cabin to write down what I'd just learned about my job. I felt pretty confident about my knowledge and ability to handle horses but I still didn't know what "wrangle" meant. I'd find out soon enough.

****

Two of Glenn's longtime pack-trip guides, Jack Danielson and Jerry Prince had arrived to shoe horses all day. However, it looked like it would continue to rain, so they hooked the large horse trailer to their pickup instead. They would drive to Montana and bring back another load of horses to get shoed, groomed, and guest ready.

Rimrock used to have a horse roundup in the spring and employees and volunteers would help drive the herd 100 miles from their winter pasture in Montana to the ranch in Wapiti. They would drive them down Sheridan Avenue (the main street) in Cody creating an annual tourist attraction. Unfortunately, after a fifty mile strip of Montana highway was paved along their route, Glenn decided it was too hard on the horses' hooves and legs—too many lame horses. They now hauled them in trailers. It was nowhere near as exciting.

Glenn told the wranglers that the guests had decided not to ride today as long as it kept raining. They would entertain themselves in the recreation room playing pool or ping-pong this morning.

The rain continued.

"The ranch's yellow Suburban will load up at 2:00 to take you into Cody to the Buffalo Bill Historical Center for the afternoon. Pat, you'll drive." Alice announced at lunch. I thought, good; at least I'm being productive.

And the rain continued.

When the spring rains fall in Wyoming, it's cold. Razan had shed his winter coat and with no place to get undercover, he was standing with his head down, back hunched up, and shivering. I felt sorry for him. I'd gotten him into this and it was up to me to help him out. I decided that I would purchase a waterproof blanket for him while I was in town.

I told the boys at the lunch table what I planned to do. After they got through snickering, (I guessed no one blanketed horses in the west) Rand told me to go to Corral West. "Not the store on Sheridan, but the outlet near the post office on the way to the airport. They have a better selection of ranch supplies." I figured I'd found my way 2500 miles from Maine, I could find the Corral West outlet, after I found Cody and the museum.

Cody was the epitome of what a modern western town ought to be and that is—not "touristy". It looked like, and was, a real functioning western town, pop around 8000. Although Cody was the largest city and county seat of Park County, its residents were down-home friendly, even to strangers.

The first attraction after passing the Buffalo Bill Reservoir, Dam, and Shoshone Power Plant, was the Cody Nite Rodeo. Opening night was next week, June 1 and the whole ranch attended every Thursday night. I couldn't wait; ya-hoo and yee-haw, I'd never seen a real live rodeo.

After passing a few motels, restaurants, and an attraction called Old Trail Town (I'd have to check that out later), I spotted the Buffalo Bill Historical Center. I pulled into the parking lot to let the guests out and said, "I'll be parked right around here and we'll head back to the ranch promptly at 4:30."

I found the Corral West outlet, after a fashion, and purchased a horse blanket for Razan. I was back to the center in time to do a little touring myself. I read the center's directory, which included the Buffalo Bill Museum, Whitney Gallery of Western Art, Plains Indian Museum, Cody Firearms Museum and the Harold McCracken Research Library. The complex was a collection of four excellent museums under one roof. I went to the Indian section first then wandered around the western art gallery. I looked at my watch and it was almost 4:30. Shoot, I thought, guess I'll have to tour here again on another rainy day. Time to go.

****

Well, Rimrock's corral now supported the only bright-blue blanketed horse in Wapiti, maybe in all Wyoming. I smiled at the absurdity of it all and knew neither Glenn or the other wranglers would let me forget this, but I was genuinely pleased with the result. With his waterproof cover, though he sure was noticeable, even to the other horses, Razan was warm, dry and eating again.

CHAPTER 7

Usually Tuesday meant everyone got up early to ride to an outdoor cowboy breakfast. However, it was still raining so the ranch went to a "Plan B", which was to have a cookout in the front yard and eat on the covered porch. Glenn still served up his blueberry hotcakes, and everyone was happy.

After breakfast, Glenn assigned me the job of making a large 3-foot x 4-foot horse chart on an erasable board that would hang in the saddling area. I listed all the horses' and mules' names leaving two blank spaces next to each. Glenn or Tom would fill in the name of whoever was assigned to that horse and their saddle number. Everyone could use the chart to see what horses were being used, by whom, and which ones were available.

The rain had finally stopped. Alice announced the guests would be taking the usual ranch sponsored river "float trip" that afternoon. I was to drive the guests into Cody, again, and escort them, with the Wyoming River Trip guides, down the Shoshone on rafts. The river trip was in moderate white water with class II rapids. It would be cold this time of year, exciting, but relatively safe for all ages.

The Wyoming River Trip guides transported all guests via busses from their office in the Holiday Inn complex to the

Shoshone River near the old DeMaris Hot Springs. I smelled the offensive sulfur odor from the Hot Springs but kept my comments to myself.

The other seven guests as well as myself got wet when we hit the "washing machine" and the "little Colorado" rapids, but dried off while drifting through the Red Rock Canyon. One lady dropped her paddle and reached for it just as we hit the "roller coaster". She fell over the side but a fast-acting guide pulled her back into the raft in a hurry. I was having a great time—and getting paid for it. However, I wondered if I was ever going to get to "wrangle," whatever that was.

Upon returning to the rafting headquarters, everyone changed into dry clothes and waited to collect their rafting pictures that the company had taken during their fun river trip.

While the guests and I were in Cody, another wrangler arrived at the ranch. Grady drove all the way from Utah in his beat-up old truck. He was a student at Brigham Young University studying Theology to become a Mormon minister. He claimed to be an experienced horseman.

How much Grady, or I, knew about being a wrangler would soon be tested.

The forecast for the remainder of the week was for clear skies; guests would definitely be riding. The head wrangler Tom said, "Pat and Grady, you'll wrangle tomorrow. I kept Beauty in the corral for you to ride, Pat. Grady, you'll ride Reno."

Jerry was going to be around shoeing horses all day and I was thankful when he volunteered to accompany us *novices*. He would ride Cowtown, the horse he always used as his guide horse on pack trips.

Beauty was a spirited black mare of average build, about 15.3 hands, who loved to race. Grady, Jerry and I set off across

Canyon Creek and took the trail winding up the left side of the bluff. About ten minutes into the ride Jerry spotted a small group of 12-15 horses and said he would round them up and take them back to the ranch himself. He said that when we came upon the main bunch, one wrangler should act as herd leader and ride in front, while the other person rounded up the strays and pushed the bunch to follow the leader.

Grady and I reached the crest and spotted the herd scatted all over the flat top. I galloped Beauty toward the headwall intending to lead the horses around the steep slope of the bluff and come into the ranch corrals from the side. The horses, being more familiar with the wrangle routine than I, took control and decided to go straight to the ranch, over the headwall, at a gallop. At that point, I had two choices: I could wimp out, going around the slope and coming in a half-hour after the herd arrived, or I could go for it and gallop down over the headwall with the rest. I decided to go for it; hoped Beauty could handle it; and said a silent prayer before hurdling over the brim.

All horse lovers have seen or read *The Man from Snowy River* and his big scene chasing "brumbies" down the mountain. Well, to me, this was exactly the same scenario. Beauty, as well as the other horses, leaped over the brim, slid on their haunches or galloped sideways until reaching the bottom a couple hundred feet below. Was I scared—no; was I thrilled—yes.

Grady wasn't far behind. A few of the older horses had taken the switchback trail rather than gallop down the headwall and after they were all in, Grady closed the corral gate and he and I went to breakfast. No one said anything about our downhill gallop so I figured it was a normal event in wrangling and I didn't mention it to anyone.

Later in the week, however, I overhead Grady as he expounded to Jerry about how exciting and dangerous it was galloping the horses down the headwall. Jerry said he wished he'd returned to help us. "Sounds like I missed a once in a lifetime ride," he said. Only then did I realize that this incident was very much out of the normal realm of wrangling and I should be proud of myself. I was becoming a real cowgirl.

I later discerned that because of Beauty's tendency to race, she was not used as a wrangle horse. Tom must have known this and had intentionally put me on her thinking, hoping, I couldn't handle her. This would have served to show that I couldn't do the job. What a jerk! Maybe that's why he was gone within the next week, either fired or quit. I didn't care. Glenn appointed Rand to be the head wrangler again for this year. I was happy with the choice. I liked Rand; he had integrity.

CHAPTER 8

When Glenn suggested I take the afternoon off, I was delighted. I had kept my horse in the corrals instead of sending him out to pasture hoping that I'd get a chance to ride this week.

Debby and Ann had approached me earlier and asked if they could ride with me sometime. Being equestriennes, they came to be employed at the ranch thinking they'd get to do some horse back riding, then learned that they could ride *only* if there were horses available *and* a wrangler willing to escort them. At this time of year, *horses* were available to ride and *I* had some spare time to escort.

They wanted to ride to the pastures near the highway to do some loping. This was fine with me as I hadn't ridden in that area yet. After a nice lope over the grassy meadows, Debby looked up and said, "Look at that building up there that resembles a Chinese pagoda. Let's ride up the hill to see it."

I found a trail that led up from the pastures and went passed the pagoda. What an odd looking structure, I thought. Rumor was that a man built it for his lover; when scorned, he hanged himself. The building now stands empty. How sad!

We trotted along a grass-filled road, which lead to a sign saying Green Creek Road. Following that dirt road, we passed a rock wall containing some kind of hieroglyphics. I would have to find out what those were about so I could inform guests. Eventually the road led across the creek which I recognized from my ride with Tom. I knew my way back to the ranch from there. Nice ride; good company. We agreed to ride together again and explore up Canyon Creek.

****

Glenn told me my next day off wasn't until Sunday, so I asked him if I could turn Razan out with the herd at night instead of his remaining in the corral. Glenn said, "If you think Raisin can handle the wrangle back and forth, you can try it this evening when the wranglers take the horses to the front pasture."

It didn't turn out exactly as planned. At first, Razan was excited to be running free with the herd, but after a mile, he turned around and ran back to the corral. Razan wanted food and to him the corral was where he'd been fed. After a good laugh at his individuality, I "ponied" him beside Navaho to the horse pasture. When he found good grass to eat there, he was content to stay.

For the remainder of the week, the wranglers wormed horses, cut bridle paths, and picked tails, while Tom lead the seven guests on local trail rides around the ranch.

The next week Tom left, so Rand and Cole took turns leading the twelve guests on trail rides. When they weren't leading rides, Rand and Cole helped Glenn and Grady finish clearing debris from the horse trails. Travis got the job of digging and unblocking irrigation ditches while Sean, Jack, and Jerry shoed the remaining barefoot horses.

I drove the guests into Cody again Tuesday and Wednesday to the museum and float trip, though I didn't do the trips myself.

I became familiar with the city and now knew where the post office, grocery store, best art galleries, souvenir shops, and clothing shops were.

In between guest trips to Cody, I checked fences on horseback and made necessary repairs. I carried the wire cutters, claw hammer, and fencing staples in a leather saddlebag thrown over the back of a buckskin named Taxi, who was content to graze nearby as I mended fences.

Another new wrangler, Petre Piuci, arrived during the week. He was a veterinary student from Northern Italy and was as handsome as they come. He had beautiful eyes and a naive smile that could melt the hearts of ladies from five to seventy-five. The guest ladies and girls would love him. He'd be good for business.

Rand, Sean, Cole, and Travis occupied the four-man side of a bunkhouse; Petre moved into the smaller two-man side with Fred. Sean, Petre and Fred all played guitar and sang country/western songs and on many evenings their music soothed the ranch to sleep.

Glenn free-leased three young Appaloosas that summer, under the condition that only wranglers ride and train them. Petre chose a handsome sorrel Appaloosa with a white blanket, named Clyde, for his wrangle horse. I picked a beautiful dark gray three-year-old Arab/Appy named Washakie to train and use as my extra guide horse. The third Appy was a waste of time and money. The wranglers gave up trying to teach him anything.

****

The boys were horsing around roping each other down by the corrals one evening after supper. I got my arms roped to my sides by Travis; then Rand threw a rope and caught one of my feet. They were about to hog-tie me when I yelled, "Stop. Can you teach me to throw a lasso so I can defend myself?"

The boys all raised their eyebrows.

"Sure, I can show you how; watch," Rand said, "then practice for a few years."

Rand held the lariat loop with his right hand at his side, brought it across his front to his left, up his left shoulder, circled his head to his right shoulder, then threw it out and down over a stump.

I tried the same thing a couple of times before I got the hang of it and got the loop out into the air. I tried it several more times and finally managed to get the loop over a corral post.

"Guess I won't be roping a moving horse anytime soon," I said, annoyed at myself.

"Don't worry about roping horses," Rand replied, "we only do that when Chief is around." He explained that loops whirling in the air upset the horses and made them hard to catch. It was also dangerous for wranglers to be in the small corral with 40-50 horses running and bumping into each other.

I decided I'd be content to rope a good-looking wrangler.

CHAPTER 9

Business picked up the next week with 20 guests. By mid-June, there were 28 and now, the last week of June, business was booming with 40 guests. Between cabin girls, waitresses, maintenance man, yard boy, cooks, wranglers and guides, there were 23 employees.

Rand, as head wrangler, assigned wrangle partners: he and Grady, Cole and Sean, Petre and I. I was really happy to have Petre as my partner for the summer. Together we vetted the sick and injured horses, and took special care of the very young and the very old. He was kind to animals. I liked that.

Partners wrangled every three days so I only had to rise early and round up the horses twice a week. That wasn't too bad. I liked to lead the herd and Petre had the fun of rounding them up. He got all the dust in his face but said he didn't mind. I figured he was being nice.

As a mountain wrangler, Travis helped Jerry get the black packhorses and camp gear ready for pack trips that would start July 1st. The pack horses Elvira, Ellie, and sisters Dolly and Molly, were gorgeous black Percherons with abundant manes, long forelocks over wide foreheads, lively eyes, long necks, and powerful forearms and thighs. They looked as if "Armor-plated Knights of the Middle Ages should be riding them into battle". Heavily built Ebony, Sambo, Sankey, Satan and Nemo made up the remainder of The Black pack string. Fred was their pack cook.

The head guide, Jack, had hired a mountain wrangler, Greg. Together with Jack's wife, Kyla, who was their pack cook, they pack tripped with Glenn's string of ten white mules. They were busy readying the mules, tents and camping equipment for weekly mountain trips in July and August. Rimrock's white mules were rare and famous. They'd been the lead attraction in Cody's Fourth of July Parade for many years.

****

This weekend was Cody's Annual Plains Indian Powwow, sponsored by the Buffalo Bill Historical Center, and set up on the south end of its parking lot. Cheyenne, Comanche, Kiowa, Crow, Blackfeet, and Sioux, along with Arapaho, Apache, Navaho, Shoshone, Nez Perce', Ute and Pawnee tribes were represented.

Visitors from far and near, including Rimrock Ranch guests and workers, were drawn to the rainbow of colors and the Indians singing and dancing to the rhythmical beating of drums. Many special activities like hoop, snake, and owl dances added to the festivities of the weekend.

I drove into Cody on Sunday morning and wondered at the enormity of the crowd enjoying the powwow as I tried to find a parking spot nearby. I marveled at the explosion of colored beadwork of red, yellow, orange, blue, green and purple, and the feather-work of the "fancy" dancers. The honored "traditional" dancers followed, adorned in black and white feathers, carrying the flags of two worlds, portraying the warriors of old in their classic dance movements. The "traditional shawl women" dancers and the younger children paraded into the arena next.

On the outskirts of the dance arena, booths selling Indian beads, jewelry, clothing, and accessories were set up for visitors to purchase.

****

During the week, I drove guests into Cody less frequently now, as each of us six wranglers took turns driving. More guests also meant all activities and trail rides went as scheduled. We wranglers were busy.

Every morning after breakfast, except Sunday, wranglers headed for the corrals to get our horses and the guest horses ready to ride. Today was Monday and I was guiding the Introductory Ride with Razan. I pulled him out of the corral first and tied him to a rail. When the rest of the herd was run into the small round corral it was real tight quarters and too easy for a new horse to be kicked or bitten by more aggressive horses.

Rand was busy writing each guest's name and saddle number beside their assigned horse on the chart that I had made. He yelled to me across the saddling area, "Did you notice Two Tone still limping when you wrangled this morning? He's supposed to be assigned to Marion for the week."

"Yes, he was," I replied. "Maybe we can put her on Arapaho? Still a paint, same disposition."

"Probably, but hold up on catching either one until I check with Chief. Sean, here's the list of the horses we need for this week. Grady, you start putting out saddles. Pat, you start grooming. I'll be right back to help saddle." With that, Rand headed up to the ranch house.

Sean, Cole, and Petre were busy catching and haltering horses, then bringing them to the gate for me. I led them, two at a time, to the hitching rails. Cole said, "Be careful with Bonfire and Macho. They're "pullbacks" so make sure they're not tied when you work around them or they may panic and pull on their lead rope until they break something, i.e. their halter, or a hitching post."

"Thanks for the heads-up. Do I tie them at all?" I asked.

"Bonfire gets tied to the tree next to the saddle shed and just flip Macho's lead rope over the rails; he'll stay okay," Cole replied.

When I had a dozen horses tied to the rails I got out the currycomb and brushes, and started grooming. When there were 20 or more horses to groom I just cleaned the strategic areas, being under the saddle and girth, and barely touched their rump, neck or legs unless they were really dirty—it took too much time.

Rand was back and okayed substituting Arapaho for Two Tone. He said, "Grady, are you riding Adobe again today?"

"Yes, I love that big guy and want him for my wrangle horse."

"Ok, then you'd better go catch him yourself because the boys can't seem to get him.

"Sean, would you come finish putting out the saddles?"

With only a few more horses to catch, Cole suddenly said, "Here comes Chief."

"Then lets rope these last ones, get out of there, and everyone start saddling."

After grooming, two saddle pads are placed on the horses back, with the fleece pad nearest their hide. Saddles are checked for proper fit and breast collars are attached to the saddles. Cinches are pulled just tight enough to enable the saddles to stay on. They are pulled tighter just before guests mount up. Bridles are fitted and put on over the horses' halters. Snaffle bits with shanks and curb straps are used on all guest horses, and most wrangle horses as well.

Nine o'clock arrived, as did the guests; there were still horses being saddled. Glenn said for Rand and Cole to come help get guests mounted, while Grady, Sean, Petre, and I finished saddling the horses. On an average, each wrangler saddled and bridled seven to nine horses each morning.

I usually tried to saddle the small and medium-size horses, but occasionally I was stuck saddling a tall one. I was always thankful when Rand came around to lift a heavy man's saddle onto a tall horse for me. Later in the summer, I found I could lift any saddle onto any horse.

The introductory ride followed the same trail as Razan and I had explored my first Sunday at the ranch. Once groups of ten to twelve guests were mounted, Glenn gave them basic instructions in the small corral on reining their horse left, right, and to "Whoa." Rand chose one wrangler to lead the group and another to ride last to be sure everyone was keeping up. Glenn watched them closely as they left the corral to make sure the guests could handle their horses satisfactorily. I led my group with Razan. Whereas he'd walked this trail before, he acted like he was a seasoned guide horse.

Soon all guests and wranglers were on the trail. This first ride had all levels of riders on it so we walked, got used to the horses, and enjoyed the scenery. No moose or deer; too much noise. We stopped for a rest at the apex, the same as I had done. It was the proverbial picture taking spot.

When the last group made it back to the saddling area, the wranglers loosened all the horses' saddle cinches and put grain-filled feedbags on them, giving additional amounts to the aging horses.

At lunch, Glenn announced that all guests would be taking a three-hour trail ride in the afternoon, meeting at the saddling area at 1:00. Everyone was to ride in one big group. Whereas only five wranglers were needed, Glenn told me to take the afternoon off. Gladly, I thought. I've been up since 6:00 am; rode for four miles before breakfast wrangling horses; groomed 30 horses; saddled 7 of them; and led a morning trail ride.

I took a nap.

CHAPTER 10

Square dancing was in the Ramuda (recreation) Room every Monday evening and *all* employees participated per orders of the Chief. Glenn called the dancing to old 78-rpm records playing western music. There were "circle" dances, where everyone changed partners on each round and "square" dances", where partners got to swing with other partners. On the old time Virginia Reel and Lady of The Lake, ladies and gentlemen got to swing or dosey-doe until their heads reeled. Maybe it was the absurdity of it all, or the fact that it put young and old, male and female, on the same level. Whatever it was, everyone had fun, much to our surprise. It was a wonderful way to mix guests and employees; and Glenn, being the all-knowing wise Chief, knew how to host a good time.

By the time the dancing ended at 9:30, I was glad I'd taken a nap because I was tired again. Glenn announced that all guests had to be at the corral at 7:30 the next morning. Everyone was riding to breakfast! That meant wranglers needed to start saddling by 6:00 am. Well, I thought, at least *I* don't have to get up that early and wrangle tomorrow.

Blueberry pancakes, here we come. The guests were mounted and wranglers intermingled in the line of forty horses and riders. Rand led the group; I was riding about six horses back. I was just starting to cross Canyon Creek when Navaho stumbled and went down on his knees into the water. I stayed on, pulled up on the reins to help him get back on his feet, and off we went again as if nothing happened, except my feet were now soaked. Rand yelled back, "Hey Pat, you okay? Or are you just entertaining the guests this morning?"

"Yes, I'm okay," I replied to his jest. "I didn't have time to shower this morning so I thought I'd get wet in the creek instead."

We climbed switchbacks up steep slopes then headed into the forest following the trail along Green Creek a couple of miles before the aroma of bacon and coffee filled the air. There in a small meadow, Glenn and his helper Fred cooked over a campfire. Coffee was ready.

While the wranglers tied, hobbled, and let other horses graze freely, the guests "chowed down" on blueberry hot cakes, eggs and bacon, with orange juice on the side. Tales of Navaho's not-so-graceful trip through the creek was retold a few time, as well as rumors of Cole's spotting mountain lion spoor during Monday's ride up the Canyon. Mountain lions are notoriously illusive so there was no way a wrangler or guest was going to see one, but Cole confirmed that the tracks were fresh. Soon the big cats would head for higher summer hunting grounds.

The large group split into three smaller groups on the ride back to the ranch. One group of novices and walkers would return via the same route as we came up.

A second group took a longer round-a-bout route down Green Creek Road. When we got to some level ground, we trotted the horses for a while before heading back down the trails to the ranch.

The third group started on the same road as the second, then the roughnecks, rowdies, and daredevils veered off and headed up a sagebrush hill. When they reached the top, Rand and Grady told everyone that they could ride back down to the road as fast as they wanted. No trail, just rocks of various sizes, gully-wales, a few small fir trees, and lots of sagebrush in the way.

Rand yelled, "Last one to the bottom buys drinks," and off he and Grady raced.

Guests tried to follow; some made it, breathless but intact; while others were totally unprepared to ride off-trail, at a fast pace, downhill, and ended up in the sagebrush. No one was hurt, and for some, it was their riding highlight of the week. It gave them bragging rights because they'd done something the other guests didn't do.

After lunch, Sean and Cole drove the vans into Cody. While the guests went rafting, they met in the park and caught a couple hours of sleep under the shade trees. It was Grady's and Rand's afternoon off and they'd gone to visit Rand's parents.

Petre and I stayed at the ranch and doctored the two horses in the hospital pasture. Buck had a stick puncture in his left hindquarter that Petre cleaned out, stitched up, and then gave him a shot of antibiotics. Coke had gravel in the sole of his right front hoof. His cornet band was swollen with inflammation. I soaked it with warm water and Epsom Salts to help bring out the abscess. I'd have to continue soaking his hoof daily for the next week to see results. In the meantime, he hobbled on three legs, as he couldn't put weight on that hoof.

****

There was still a couple of hours until supper so I saddled Razan and went for a late afternoon ride up into the Canyon. I hadn't gone more than a half mile beyond the creek when my horse stopped suddenly. I looked ahead and saw what appeared to be a large dog in the trail. Upon second glance, I could see it was a bear squatting. Each stared at one another for a few seconds, then not knowing what to do, I headed back to the ranch to tell Chief. Razan was anxious but didn't seem scared. Probably there were so many different scents around that the bear's smell didn't stand out.

"Chief, I just saw a bear on the trail not far past the creek."

"Must be a young adult brown bear who's just been kicked out of the den by his mother who has a new cub. They wander around for a while not knowing what to do or where to go. They're usually harmless, but go tell the boys to run it up into the Canyon," Glenn said, "and don't let the guests know about it or they'll be chasing the bear all over the ranch and someone will get hurt."

I rode to the corral where Petre was cleaning his saddle and Rand and Grady were just ready to wrangle the horses back to pasture.

"Hey guys, there's a bear up on the Canyon Trail and Chief said to head it back up into the Canyon before it gets any closer. And don't alarm the guests."

"Petre throw your saddle on Fiddler," said Rand, "Lets go boys, we'll follow you, Pat."

Great, I thought, Razan was real good the first time; wonder what his reaction to the bear will be second time around.

The bear wasn't on the trail where I had first seen him but Grady spotted it down by the creek. The boys went galloping after it whooping and yelling, "Ya-hoo" and "Yee-haw." Look out bear, I thought. I'll bet it won't be back to this ranch for awhile.

Razan was excited now; not so much by the bear, but the yelling, running, and hollering was beyond his comprehension.

He couldn't decide whether to run with the other horses or run away from all the noise. Not wanting to press my luck, I turned him back to the ranch.

CHAPTER 11

Did you ever see softball players in cowboy boots and hats? It's a hilarious sight. Rimrock employees and guests played ball every Wednesday morning in a sagebrush and cactus field. And yes, wranglers wore their cowboy boots and hats. Glenn picked the captains, who in turn chose players, and the game was on.

Whoever chose Cole had a definite advantage as he'd played some minor league baseball and compared to the rest of us, he was awesome. I played softball in a women's league years ago so I was familiar with the game. I played roving shortstop for the ranch and even made a few good hits during the summer, much to the other wranglers' surprise. Of course I tripped over sagebrush and got "thorned" by prickly pear a few times, but so did everyone else. It was all part of the game.

Not every rule was fair. Chief umpired and gave the youngest kids unlimited strikes until they finally hit the ball. He called fair balls, *out*, on the winning team if they were too far ahead. All the rule bending eliminated the chance of hard feelings, except for Grady, who had to keep his temper in check if his team lost.

Back at the ranch, Alice said The Wapiti Lodge had called saying some horses were grazing on the side of the highway nearby. She had driven down and determined that seven of the mountain horses had escaped through an old pasture gate. All six of us saddled up and headed out to round up the wandering strays before they got hit by a car.

When a few like-employees get together on their own, sometimes they become inventive—too inventive, maybe. As we wranglers loped up and down slopes, galloped across pastureland, and leaped irrigation ditches, there was bound to be competition going on. Too much testosterone dictated that someone had to be the fastest.

Grady hollered over to Cole, "Race you to the highway gate."

Cole replied, "Eat my dust." And the race was on, Cole riding Cody and Grady riding Adobe. The rest brought up the rear but weren't far behind. We knew Chief would never approve of racing; Rand only hoped neither our horses nor we got injured in the folly.

No one was at the highway gate to call a winner and, of course, neither would concede defeat. They were going to race again, with the wranglers at the finish line this time, when Sean said, "There're the horses up there near The Red Barn."

Quietly we rode up to the strays. Rand roped Zane and began leading him alongside the highway. The rest of us surrounded the other horses on three sides and moved them in behind Zane being careful to keep them out of traffic. This sight provided a photo opportunity for tourists; many cars stopped to take pictures—real wranglers, real horses.

****

Wednesday afternoon's "wine and cheese" ride was a three-hour ride. The trail began at the driveway opposite the yearling's pasture then climbed about a third of the way up and around the side of The Rim, crossing some ledges that looked down on the highway. I was astride Navaho and held my breath while riding over the ledges hoping that he wouldn't choose this place to stumble again. I'd lost some faith in him but came to learn that he didn't stumble in strategic places, only when he wasn't paying attention.

The trail descended a bank into the West Fork of Canyon Creek and then followed the creek for a couple miles before the riders stopped. Everyone rested in a small grove under evergreen trees, drank a small cup of wine, and ate cheese and crackers.

After remounting, the riders climbed semi-steep switchbacks up the backside of the canyon rim. The guests didn't know that the wine was to help make them mellow for their ride down the other side.

As I stood at the top looking down, I said to Rand, who was standing nearby, "Don't tell me *that's* the trail we have to descend."

"It's the easiest of two trails. Don't worry, the horses know how to descend, if the guests let them alone."

With that, Rand gave the guests some riding instructions. "The horses know how to step down from cliff to cliff and rock to rock. They are familiar with the trail, so *do not* try to tell them how to go down. Let them do it themselves. You just sit balanced and lean back just a bit to help. Don't hold the reins too tight, the reins are not brakes."

And down they went, faces white, no talking, no picture taking, silence, concentrating, mostly scared. Guests have wet themselves on that ride down The Rim.

In mid-summer, I initiated a very successful alternative "soda pop" ride for the not-so-brave, over near the East Branch of Canyon Creek. We'd stop for soda pop in an area where many old animal bones could be found and the wranglers would give prizes for the most bones found and the largest. As the guests couldn't carry most bones back with them, the last wrangler stayed behind and scattered the bones back around the woods, to be found by next week's guests.

****

Jim Bama, a distinguished artist and friend of the Fales' who lived in Wapiti, was a guest at dinner that evening. He'd painted a large picture of Phyllis and a Cowboy that hung in the ranch dining room and had exhibits in the Western Art Museum in Cody. Everyone feasted on roast pork, mashed potatoes, applesauce, carrots and peas, my favorite meal. Mr. Bama stayed through the evening's cowboy sing-a-long, featuring Petre, Fred and Sean.

I slipped away from the sing-a-long as soon as I'd heard Petre sing *Old Paint* and Fred's rendition of *Desperado*. I went back to my cabin to sleep—I thought. Unfortunately, a mouse decided to share my room and disrupt my sleep by running up my arm. The boys had been having trouble with mice in their room and I suspected Rand was instrumental in putting this one in mine. I pulled the covers over my head to keep the too-friendly mouse off my body and decided that tomorrow I'd think of some way to get back at Rand, and ask Fred to de-mouse my room.

The next morning it was my turn to wrangle so I got to the wrangle shed a little earlier than necessary. I had thought of a way to get back at Rand for his "mouse-trick." I would "short-stirrup" his saddle. It's similar to short-sheeting a bed: the near stirrup is left alone, when Rand swings his right leg over the saddle, he'll find the off-stirrup above his knee, instead of down by his foot.

When it was time to begin the ride, Rand mounted up, and in front of waiting guests, he had to dismount, go to the horse's off-side to adjust his right stirrup, and mount up again. He looked disgruntled and a little embarrassed, but never said a word.

CHAPTER 12

I had saddled Razan to ride to Table Mountain on the "all-day" ride. I was at the end of the line, and as it turned out, I was lucky to be there. A pack animal always accompanied the riders on Thursdays to carry soda pop and food to be cooked over an open fire for lunch.

Petre had packed Pecos today. Pecos was a bay mustang, formerly a wild horse rounded up and sold to Rimrock. He was not a guest horse as he was apt to be spooky. I owned Arabs—I knew spooky. I had ridden Pecos as a guide horse and found him surefooted and willing to lead, although a little flighty. He was *never* supposed to be a pack animal. Can you imagine a spooky horse with pack gear strapped to his back? Not a good idea!

Rand was nearly up to the first switchback, guests were just crossing Canyon Creek, when pandemonium ensued. Something in Pecos' pack had started rattling while he was crossing the creek and that's all it took for him to panic. He tore his lead rope away from Petre and went bucking and charging through the guests and horses in front of him, scattering them down the creek bank to the left and up the slope to the right.

Horses kicking, rearing, people falling off, screaming. What a fiasco! It was funny when relating it around the campfire later over lunch, but at the time, it was total chaos. Petre returned to the corrals and with Jerry's help, packed up the mule, Jeff.

The Table Mountain riders had just passed the breakfast area when Petre and the pack mule caught up. The group crossed Green Creek then started to climb. After a couple hours in the saddle, we reached a level spot and took a fifteen-minute rest stop for horses and guests.

Petre led the pack mule past the guests and continued to travel on alone. He planned to have the fire going and hot coffee for the guests when they reached Table Mountain. The only problem was that Petre didn't realize there were two trails to the top. He took one; the rest of us took the other.

Switchbacks were getting steeper and more dangerous; trees were getting smaller; and the air was chilly, as there was still snow on the ground in places. In the distance, a strange call came from a wild animal. Razan was beginning to fret and dance around. He kept looking around, worried about something coming up behind him. He did not like being at the end of the line.

After another mile of riding through stunted conifers we arrived at the high meadow where Petre was supposed to have the fire going and coffee ready—no Petre.

Rand said, "Cole, why don't you ride up to the summit to see if Petre took the wrong trail and he's waiting for us up there."

"I hope he hasn't headed back down again," Cole replied and he went loping toward the top.

The wranglers loosened all the horses' cinches and tied their reins around their necks intertwined in the throatlatch so the reins wouldn't slip over their necks. The guest horses were let loose to graze the long meadow. The wranglers' horses (all except Razan) were tied to trees to ensure they could be caught. I knew I could catch my horse so I let him graze with the others.

I looked up and saw Cole, Petre and the pack mule coming down from the summit. "Hey, how about that warm fire and hot coffee," I said.

"If you guys had told me which trail to take it would have been ready," Petre replied.

Soon hamburgers and hot dogs were sizzling on the grill and guests and wranglers were enjoying coffee or hot chocolate.

The guests had a spectacular view while eating lunch. The ranch and all of Wapiti Valley was visible. Rand said the elevation was about 9500 feet above sea level.

After lunch and a rest, I called Razan and we rounded up the other horses. The guests re-mounted and the climb to the summit began. The horses were puffing as they climbed the last few hundred feet in the very thin air. Once on top, it was safe for groups of five or six to lope up small inclines. The theory being, at that elevation the horses weren't going to run far, and loping uphill was fairly safe as bucking was unlikely. Of course, there were always guests who loped too close to one another, even after being warned to keep a horse-distance apart, thus falling off as their horse shied away from the other's kick.

I led the way back down a different trail than we had climbed up to Table Mountain. My horse slid on his hind legs descending steep sandy banks and cautiously crossed exposed ledges, perhaps feeling my anxiety. This side of the mountain was more open and the view of Ptarmigan Mountain and Green Creek Canyon was breathtaking.

I was enjoying the scenery and the ride down when I heard Rand yell, "Hey, slow that *Arab* down a little, this isn't a race to the bottom." I hadn't noticed that Razan was hurrying and walking too fast. From then on, I stopped frequently letting the others catch up. Everyone stopped for a break at the breakfast meadow then continued back to the ranch, arriving late afternoon.

"Sean, would you wrangle for me?" I asked. "I can't wrangle with Razan and don't want to bother to catch Navaho."

"Sure if you'll wrangle for me tomorrow night. Then I can have all tomorrow afternoon and evening off."

"Deal," I replied and headed up to my cabin to change and clean up for the Cody Nite Rodeo.

While Sean and Petre were taking the horses out to pasture, mischief was in the making. Rand put a rope around the neck of a huge stuffed bear his girlfriend Tara had given him. Then he and Cole hid it behind a large rock next to the small corral. When Sean came riding back into the saddling area, they pulled the bear out from its hiding place right in front of Sean's horse. Penny, not having a tolerant disposition, spun around, bucked three times and Sean hit the ground, cussing. They all laughed and thought it was funny. When I heard about it, I thought, I don't think it's amusing at all, especially if they do that to me.

****

The all-day ride was a very long ride for youngsters and as the summer went on, Glenn and I started taking kids under ten years old on a "half-day hotdog" ride up the canyon. We took a pack mule with us just like the "big guys" and made a campfire alongside Canyon Creek. We showed the kids how to cut sticks for cooking hotdogs and marshmallows over the open fire. After lunch, Chief showed them how to have a boat race, pretending the broken sticks were boats and letting them drift down the creek.

On the way back to the ranch, Glenn pointed out a split in the trail. He said that the trail heading to the right up toward Ptarmigan Mountain led to the remains of Jeremiah Johnson's cabin. Jeremiah Johnson, being a notorious mountain man of the west, interested me. I thought, maybe this would make a good exploratory ride for Debby, Ann, and me to take the next time we rode together.

CHAPTER 13

"Let's go rodeo," was the chant as wranglers and guests, dressed in their best cowboy/cowgirl attire, loaded into waiting Rimrock vans.

Cody was often referred to as the Rodeo Capital of the World because nowhere else was a full rodeo staged nightly for three months in a row from June through August. Rodeo stock took on cowboys from across the country in bareback, saddle bronc, bull riding, calf roping, team roping and bulldogging events. Having fallen off many horses, many times in my life, I liked the saddle bronc riding the best. I could identify with their sincere desire to stay on the bucking horses and not get thrown off.

Other traditional events of the Cody Nite Rodeo included barrel racing for cowgirls and steer riding for younger cowboys. For children who attended the rodeo, there were fun events including the calf scramble and stick-horse race. Adults attending envied the crowd's adulation of the cowboys and some even fancied participating themselves. Our guests didn't know they'd get their chance on Saturday at Rimrock's Guest Rodeo.

Glenn discouraged Rimrock wranglers from participating in the rodeo as he didn't want his employees injured, mangled, mutilated or disabled. He let it be known that if you get hurt at the rodeo, you wouldn't be able to do your work and would be fired. The boys, knowing this, always sat near the chutes below the Buzzards Roost talking with the cowboys and watching them perform with envy. I had wanted to enter Phyllis in the barrel racing competition, but Chief and Alice both said an emphatic, "NO." So I sat and watched with the guests.

At half time, I was buying a drink when I ran into Dustin, who I'd met at the ranch the day I arrived.

"Howdy, ma'am. Pat isn't it?" he said. "Nice to see you again."

"Same here, are you watching or partaking?"

"Just watching tonight, although I'm entered in the Wild Horse Race here next weekend during the Cody Stampede."

"I think I've heard some of the Rimrock boys talking about entering. Apparently it's a once a year event and they're raring to try for the challenge."

"And the prize money too, I'm sure," Dustin replied. "Are you sitting with anyone, or would you like to join me in the stands?"

"I'm chaperoning the ranch guests tonight, so I'd better sit with them. But I think I'm free tomorrow evening. Are you coming into town?"

"Yep, let's meet up at Cassie's around nine. I know from experience Glenn and Alice frown on your eating out, but we could go dancing. Do you know how to do the *western swing*?"

"No, but I'm trainable and I'd like to learn. See you about nine tomorrow night then." I said, trying not to sound too enthusiastic when what I really wanted to say was, "YEESSS, I need a night out with a handsome cowboy like you."

****

Rimrock employees took turns driving the ranch vans filled with guests into Yellowstone Park on Fridays. They drove to the famous Old Faithful Geyser, Upper and Lower Falls, Artists Point, Mud Volcanoes, and viewed huge buffalo herds grazing in Hayden Valley. The kitchen prepared bag lunches for all to eat when they stopped to rest at Canyon Village.

Only a few guests stayed behind to take advantage of morning customized riding trips and free time in the afternoon. Wranglers that didn't have to drive guests usually had the afternoon off, but this afternoon Glenn had a special project for Rand, Grady, and me.

Glenn and Alice had purchased Rimrock Ranch from Earl Martin. He'd passed away a few years back requesting in his will to have his ashes spread over Rimrock's land. Mr. Martin's daughter Susan, and son-in-law Steven arrived at the ranch early Friday morning requesting Glenn's assistance. He planned for Rand, being head wrangler, Grady, studying to be a minister, and me, as public relations person, to accompany them on a ride to the top of Eagle Cliffs.

Chief and Rand selected two sure-footed horses, Hugo and Macho, for the guests to ride. Chief chose Crystal for me to ride. He said she belonged to his granddaughter and assured me she had climbed the cliffs many times. Rand and Grady rode their regular wrangle horses, King and Adobe.

The trail to and from the peak consisted of switchbacks climbing over and around exposed ledges. Eventually the trail came to a high meadow that led into the forest a few hundred yards before ending atop Eagle Cliffs. Grady said a prayer before Earl Martin's ashes were released to the wind to fall over

Rimrock's land. Susan handed the metal container to Rand; he passed it to me with a terrified look on his face as if to say, "What am I supposed to do with this?" I took a handful of ashes and threw them into the wind; Grady and Rand then did the same. None of us had realized there were bones in with the ashes of cremated remains. We thought it was a little eerie.

The ride down the switchbacks was no easier or less stressful than riding up had been. Finally, back to the ranch I breathed a sigh of relief. Riding steep inclines or declines over exposed ledges was not my idea of fun. My idea of fun would be my date with Dustin tonight.

As it turned out, some of the other employees from Rimrock were also headed to Cassie's for a little dancing. I thought it wouldn't be a bad idea to have some friends around while I was with Dustin, after all I hardly knew him. I'd changed out of my blue jeans into a denim peasant skirt with silver concho belt that showed off my slim waist. I put on my good Justin boots, a long-sleeved fringed v-neck red pullover, and silver dangle earrings. I felt confident and even got a wolf whistle from Petre.

Ann, Debby, Rand and Petre rode in my car. They said they could ride back with Cole, who was already in town. The bouncer was checking ID's and Rand wasn't yet twenty-one, Wyoming's legal drinking age. I told him I'd say I was his mother and would make sure he wouldn't drink anything alcoholic. Surprisingly, they checked *my* ID, while Rand walked right in. That caused a good laugh among our group.

The Rimrock bunch sat at one long table. I checked out the bar. There was Dustin. What a handsome hunk of cowboy he was, long legs, good build, tanned rugged face, grinning back at me.

"Howdy cowboy, buy a girl a drink?" I said, walking up to him.

"Sho' 'nough, what's your pleasure, ma'am?" he drawled.

"I'll take a Coors Light, please."

"Would you like to dance this one?" Dustin asked as the band started playing *A Country Girl Can Survive*.

"I'd love to; lead on."

We did an easy two-step around the floor; Rand gave me a "thumbs-up."

We found a small table off to the side and sat down. I learned Dustin's last name was Lee, he was 35 years old, and grew up in Montana. His parents owned a horse ranch between Belfry and Bridger, not far from the Wyoming border. They raised Quarter horses and adopted wild mustangs whenever there was a government roundup.

Dustin said he'd done some rodeo saddle bronc riding when he was younger and now sometimes did team roping with a buddy of his, but mostly watched from the stands these days. He had an easy going manner, seemed to talk straight without trying to impress me with bravado and bullshit.

Dustin said, "You ready to swing dance?"

We danced the western swing (similar to the jitterbug, only faster) to *Should've Been A Cowboy* and only bumped into one couple – Petre and Ann. We slow danced to *I Can Still Make Cheyenne*, sat a little, talked a little, drank a little, and it was nearly midnight before I knew it.

"I turn into a pumpkin at midnight," I said. "Think I'd better get back to the ranch."

Dustin walked me out to my car and asked about my plans for the upcoming Cody Stampede.

I said, "I've heard that Rimrock takes all guests and employees to the parade Thursday morning. I don't know any more than that."

"I have a pack trip leaving tomorrow," Dustin said, "but I'll be back Wednesday. I'm entered in the Wild Horse Race

Thursday afternoon at one. Could we meet somewhere after that?"

"We'll probably stay in town through the afternoon, especially if the boys are in the Wild Horse Race. If I hang with them in the chute area, can you find me there?"

"Sure will; 'till then…," he held my face in his hands and kissed me once lightly, and then again, not so lightly, encircling me with his muscular arms. Oh my, I thought, as I returned his embrace.

I was left almost speechless but managed to squeak out, "See ya," before getting in my car and driving off. I should have asked the others if they wanted a ride, but it was too late now. They'd have to ride back with Cole. I wanted some time alone with my thoughts.

CHAPTER 14

Time passed quickly for me. The ranch had a full house, 45 guests, which meant 45 horses for the wranglers to catch, groom, and saddle every day. No one would be riding this Thursday, so Alice cancelled the regular Tuesday afternoon float trip and everyone rode to Table Mountain Tuesday after eating breakfast at Green Creek.

All the talk at the ranch centered on the upcoming Cody Stampede. Everyone wanted in on the Fourth of July festivities, including me. I was looking forward to Thursday and seeing Dustin. I'd learned that Rimrock provided a picnic in the park for guests and workers after the morning parade, then employees were on their own until Friday night. Cody stayed open for forty-eight hours straight, featuring concerts and barbecues in City Park, street dancing, fireworks displayed at dusk, and of course, the Nite Rodeo. All restaurants and bars remained open. I figured Dustin and I could find a lot to do.

After an earlier than usual breakfast, Glenn called, "All aboard for the Stampede Parade," as he climbed into one of the ranch vans. A few of us opted to drive our own cars. We followed the three ranch vans, forming a caravan into Cody. Petre and Ann, not having their own vehicles, rode with me.

We found space to sit under a couple of shade trees to keep out of the hot sun and watched the parade with Rimrock guests and the other employees. The Stampede Parade was one of the best in Wyoming and highlighted Cody's special Independence Day celebration.

And what a parade is was! It began at 9:30 and took nearly two hours to parade the more than 150 entries. There was a large collection of horse-drawn carriages and wagons, and cowboys and cowgirls on horseback showing their best silver-plated saddle outfits.

"Pat, look at this Arab coming up," Cole said.

"Wow, what a gorgeous animal," I replied, as a magnificent black Arabian stallion, adorned with red tassels on his headstall, breastplate, and show blanket, pranced by leading an All-Arabian Horse Club. The Arabs paraded proudly, dressed in their native costumes.

"Too bad they don't have brains to go with their beauty," Cole said.

"Oh, you're just jealous 'cause you don't own one," I chided back.

There were mule trains, mountain men, and Indians walking or riding their painted ponies. I loved the brightly beaded Indian costumes. Antique vehicles, clowns, several bands, and numerous commercial and organizational floats, all depicting the parade theme "Heading West", marched down Sheridan Avenue.

Talk about a "photo op". I took a whole roll of pictures. I couldn't decide which entry I liked the best; each entry seemed better than the last. The other wranglers liked the cowboys roping various guests standing alongside the parade route.

After the parade, Rimrock served up a chicken barbecue with accompanying cold salads, rolls, and watermelon at one end of City Park. All the ranch guests and employees took advantage of the shade trees to eat under.

When I saw Rand, Grady, Cole and Travis get up and leave, I followed.

"Hey, you guys headed to the rodeo?" I said.

"Yeah, we have to get ready for the Wild Horse Race," Rand replied. "It begins at one."

"I'm meeting Dustin there. Can I hang out with you in the chute area?"

"Sure, follow us, we park in the contestants' lot."

During the past week, the boys had been practicing for the upcoming Wild Horse Race in their spare time. They used their own wrangle horses, which wasn't a very realistic situation as they were too well trained and cooperated too easily. The horses used for the competition were raised wild, recently off the open range, never having been touched by humans until being hog-tied, haltered, and hauled to the rodeo this week, scared and fighting.

As I understood it, the teams each consisted of three members. Cole was the anchor; he would open the chute gate and hang onto the horse's halter rope. The second member, Grady, would be the mugger, holding the horse's head in his arms trying to keep it still. The third member, Rand would strap a saddle onto the wild, bucking, scared-to-death horse, and mount him. Then he would try to ride the wild, bucking, and still scared horse to the finish line at one end of the rodeo arena.

This sounded to me like it was dangerous, exciting, and terribly abusive to horses. And my cowboy friend Dustin was also entered in this competition!

The Rimrock boys were in chute three, right in the middle of the fracas, but nearer the finish line than Dustin whose team had drawn chute six at the opposite end from the finish line. I kept a low profile as there were not many females in the competitors' area. I stayed by chute three, keeping out of the boys' way. They had drawn a large Appaloosa horse with red spots. The competition was about to begin. I held my breath.

The starter's gun sounded, the chute gates opened, and the horses broke loose into the arena, leaping high in the air, biting, kicking, and throwing themselves to the ground in their frenzied scramble to get away. The scene was exciting but sad.

Cole got rope burns; Grady got bit; the Appaloosa fell on Rand's leg pinning him to the ground for a few seconds, but he stayed on and rode across the finish line. They came in second out of six entries.

"Good job Rimrock," I cheered.

Dustin's team, situated at the far end of the arena, came in third. He'd been the anchor man holding the wild horse's rope. I hoped he hadn't been hurt. I looked around anxiously for him.

Just then, someone came up behind me and put their arm around my shoulders. "Howdy ma'am," Dustin said, "you're looking sweet; sure is nice to see you."

"Howdy yourself. I'm glad to see you survived that fiasco called a race. Are you okay?"

"Just a little dry and dirty. Hey, let me wash up a bit in the men's room, then let's go for a beer, okay?"

"Yeah, I'm thirsty too. Meet me out to my car? It's in the contestants' lot, second row back. The boys showed me where to park."

"Be there in five."

Dustin and I found parking space outside the Silver Dollar Bar. The bar and restaurant had swinging doors just like an old western saloon. I thought I'd just regressed to the nineteenth century. I hoped it didn't come equipped with a "shootout" et al.

"So what's on the agenda for the rest of the afternoon?" Dustin asked, after he'd ordered a couple of beers.

"The Rimrock gang wants to meet at five for an old-time photo to give to Alice and Glenn. The place is somewhere on East Sheridan. Do you know where it is?"

"I think it's a temporary setup down by the Olde General Store. It's almost 4:30, do you want to head down that way after we finish these beers?"

"Yes, if you don't mind. I'd like to have my picture taken with the rest of the gang, for posterity and such. I understand we get dressed up in old western-style clothes and everything, to make it authentic looking."

"Sounds like a plan, let's do it."

CHAPTER 15

Nineteen Rimrock employees gathered to have our old-time photo taken in period costumes. Fred dressed like a dandy, Kyla, a madam, and Marla, a woman of wealth. Several of the boys dressed as mountain men with fake rifles and fur hats. Petre and Rand were gunslingers. Most of the ladies were in barroom attire of varying degrees of décolletage. I wore an old-fashion wedding dress with wide-brimmed hat decorated with flowers.

The evening was hot and the photographer took a long time taking 20 different pictures with an antique camera. While we stood in our group pose, the boys behind Debby, who wore a skimpy red dance-hall dress, kept slipping the straps off her shoulders or partially unzipping her dress. This was all in fun as everyone was clothed in his or her regular clothes underneath. They were just teasing her. The photos were awesomely authentic looking.

Dustin stayed through the photo session, enjoying the banter and chiding going on. He knew most of Rimrock boys and some of the females. When everyone finally had their own photograph, he said, "I'm really hungry, Pat, do you want to walk up to The Irma for dinner?"

"Yes, I'm hungry too. I've never eaten there but I've heard it's beautiful inside."

The Irma Restaurant and Hotel, called the "Grand Old Lady of Cody", was built in 1902 by Buffalo Bill for his daughter Irma. The Hotel renovated its fifteen original suites, blending Victorian furnishings and western memorabilia with the modernism of TV and AC.

After Dustin and I filled out plates from the restaurant's fabulous hot and cold buffet, I looked around and noticed the ornate, cherry-wood bar that ran the length of the restaurant. "Look at that grand bar with the mirrors running behind it. It's magnificent. Is it original?" I said.

"Yes," Dustin replied, "historians claim it was built in France and was a gift from Queen Victoria to Buffalo Bill."

I envisioned myself transported back in time again, surrounded by dance hall girls, gamblers and gunslingers. I felt right at home.

"I've got to shake down some of this scrumptious dinner. What say we take in the street dance up to the Eastgate Shopping Center? The feature band is Chris LeDoux's Saddle Boogie Band. I kinda fancy his music and would like to do a little two-stepping to it. How about you?"

"Lead on, you're the guide."

I hoped Sean and Petre were here somewhere to see and hear their mentor play at the street dance. I didn't know if they'd stayed in town or had gone back to the ranch; I'd lost track of the other employees. I was on my own now.

I felt relatively safe. I reasoned Glenn wouldn't have kept Dustin on as a guide for three years if he wasn't of reputable character. I'd also learned more about him during our conversations today, like he'd been engaged once, but never married. He said he had more things to do before he settled down. He intended to run his own pack trips a few more years, then take over his parent's horse ranch to breed, raise and train Quarter horses. Seemed like a good plan to me.

****

The shopping center's street dance was packed. Chris LeDoux and the Saddle Boogie Band had just come on stage to rousing cheers and applause. Although he was a major country music star, he was also a down-home country boy and a household name in Wyoming.

Chris began by playing his song *She's Tough* and was soon singing his recent hit *Haywire*. When the band started playing the song I was most familiar with, his duet with Garth Brooks, *Whatcha' Gonna Do With A Cowboy,* I was dancing in Dustin's arms in seventh heaven. I began to wonder, "What *am* I going to do with this cowboy?"

Dustin, also charmed by the music, held me close and as if reading my mind, said, "Do you want to leave here and find someplace we can be alone?"

The time had come for me "to do or not to do". I decided I was a big girl, could handle most situations, and I'd go as far as this would lead.

I said simply, "Yes."

"If you have in mind the same thing I have in mind, we could go back to my cabin in Pahaska. But, a better idea might be to stay here in town at the Big Bear, or nearer your ranch at the Wapiti Lodge. What do you think?"

"I don't have to be back to work until tomorrow night, so let's stay right here in town."

While Dustin checked us into the motel, I was quiet. I hoped I was making the right decision. I soon realized I had.

He kissed me as we stepped inside the door, cupping his hand around the back of my neck to pull my mouth against his. His lips, his tongue, his hands, emitted excitement and desire throughout my body.

I broke away gasping, "I, I need to use the ladies room… uh, do you have protection?"

He smiled and said, "Definitely."

Naked, we lay down on the bed; his body touching mine like a breeze bringing to life the surface of still water. Electricity exuded from every place his warm hands touched me. I thought, it's been way too long since I felt alive like this.

We kissed and groped and made love every which way. Fatigue set in and we lay contentedly curled next to one another until morning.

****

"So what would you like to do today?" Dustin asked as we finished eating a hearty breakfast at the Irma.

"You know, I haven't had time enough to sightsee much besides the inner loop of Yellowstone. Do you have any "must see" suggestions for a lady from the East?"

"Well, we can drive up Chief Joseph's Highway into the Sunlight Basin-Crandall area. It's about an hour northwest of here. Then we could come back through Beartooth Pass, Red Lodge and Belfry, Montana. We'd only be a few minutes from my parents' ranch. If we had time, we could stop for a visit. It's up to you."

"Let's start now and see how it goes. I need to be back to the ranch by suppertime."

I found the Chief Joseph Highway unforgettably scenic. It must be one of Cody Country's best kept secrets. I couldn't stop taking pictures; luckily, I still had plenty of film with me.

Dustin told me the highway was named for the Nez Perce' chief who in 1877 led a band out of Oregon after the U.S. government broke a treaty with the tribe to gain their gold-rich grounds. Their trek wended through Yellowstone Park, out to Clarks Fork Canyon, then north through Montana where the band was stopped near the Canadian border. "I will fight no more forever," Chief Joseph proclaimed.

Part of the road was still unpaved. Having to slow our speed created opportunities to photograph the fields of wildflowers and red chugwater rock formations from the car. We drove through Painter Canyon and continued up the highway to Dead Indian Pass. At an elevation of 8000 feet, the pass provided a dramatic view west to Sunlight Basin and north into the Clarks Fork Canyon.

We descended a series of switchbacks into the basin and crossed Sunlight Creek Bridge, the highest in Wyoming. We stopped at the overlook taking in the enormous depth of the gorge.

Dustin told me that when he was right out of college, he worked as a wrangler for an outfitter that did pack and hunting trips out of the nearby Crandall area. He said the abundance of wildlife was unprecedented outside of Yellowstone, and Crandall's Swamp Lake area was home to the beautiful trumpeter swans and rarely seen moose.

We turned right at the intersection, choosing to go east up the Beartooth Highway to Red Lodge, instead of west through Cooke City and into the North Entrance of Yellowstone.

Beartooth Pass reached an elevation of 11,000 feet, providing stunning views of mountain scenery stretching over the Shoshone and Custer National forests before dipping down into Red Lodge. We ate a late lunch at a small diner, filled up the truck up with gas, took pictures at the town's monument of Chief Plenty Coup, and set out driving back to Cody.

Upon reaching Belfry, Dustin said, "My folks' ranch is only fifteen miles from here, do you want to pay them a visit?"

"I'd love to, sometime; but it's 3:30 now and I really need to be back to the ranch before supper at 5:30. What do you think?"

"I think you're just about going to get back there in time."

"I would really like to meet your parents and see their ranch and horses. Maybe we can visit another day when we have more time. I don't want to say 'Hi' and then drive away."

"Agreed, and I'll hold you to it." Dustin replied.

The drive back to Cody took too long if I was to make it back to the ranch in time, and yet, it seemed too short, as Dustin and I would have to part. As the saying goes, "All good things must come to an end"; and I thought, this sure did feel like a *good thing.*

We stopped at the Big Bear where my car was still parked, bringing back fleeting memories of the night before. Dustin kissed me tenderly on the mouth, the eyelids, on my forehead, and held me tightly.

"I know you're really busy these days out to Rimrock and I've got pack trips every week for the next few weeks; *but* I definitely want to see you again. I've really enjoyed your company."

"Same here," I replied. "If you get time, you can call me in between trips and maybe we'll come up with something/some time that will work out for both of our schedules. The evening is the best time to catch me at the ranch. Keep in touch." I smiled, traced his lips with my fingertips, kissed him lightly, and left.

Driving to the ranch from Cody, My mind and body were suspended in time. All too soon, I would have to get organized and become a wrangler again. Until then, I couldn't stop myself from thinking: what if...?

CHAPTER 16

I had to stop thinking about the last two days with Dustin and get into the present. Vengeance was about to rear its ugly head.

I hadn't thought any more about the prospect of Rand being vindictive because of my playing the "short-stirrup" trick on him. I figured maybe all was forgiven, until I went to saddle Razan Saturday morning and NO SADDLE. I could easily have used a ranch saddle; there were at least a hundred in the saddle shed. There were kids' little dude saddles, ladies saddles with padded seats and narrow trees, and large seated saddles for men. However, being a bit stubborn, I wanted to use my own.

I looked everywhere, in every shed, building, truck, and corral. I asked the other wranglers, but only got a smirk for an answer. Finally running out of time, I said, "Okay, I give up, where is it?"

Rand innocuously pointed to the top of the wrangle shed. I went inside and looked up. There in the rafters was my saddle sitting on the highest crossbeam. There was no way I could climb up there and lift my saddle down. I had to "eat crow" and ask for help. After that, I decided to call it quits on getting even, declaring a truce with Rand.

On Saturdays, the guests had their choice of three very different rides: The Holy City Lope Ride, the Ranch Ride for novices or those who only wanted to walk, and Down The Rim Ride for the daredevils. I had opted to go with Rand, Cole and 12 guests on the Lope Ride, as I had never ridden on the other side of the Shoshone. The boys had assured me it was easy going so I'd decided to ride Razan. Sean and Grady led eight guests on the Rim Ride and Petre guided ten guests sightseeing around the ranch land.

After riding down the mile-long driveway, Rand said, "Cole and Pat, you stop traffic. I'll lead the guests and wait for you at the bridge."

I stood my horse in the middle of the highway and stopped traffic heading into Cody while Cole stopped traffic heading toward Yellowstone. Tourist usually enjoyed seeing the West in action and didn't seem to mind waiting.

The wooden planked bridge over the Shoshone River was long with no side rails. It could be dangerous if horses spooked so we all crossed in a line. Rand was in front guiding, I was in the middle of the pack, and Cole brought up the rear.

All was going well until the trail narrowed along the side of a bluff. First, the horses had to cross a small 18-inch-wide wooden footbridge over a stream that had washed away the trail. Next, they had to climb a steep 30-foot bank up to some cliffs. Razan crossed the bridge okay and scrambled up the bank, as was his usual method of climbing. Unfortunately, a mare named Dixie was ahead of him, taking her own casual time walking up the bank, and Razan bumped into her. She switched her tail to warn him to back off before she kicked him. He did and he went off-trail. He hadn't realized that *off-trail* could result in a fifty-foot slide into the Shoshone below.

Razan struggled back up onto the trail and finished climbing the bank. I could feel his heart pounding, as was mine. I gave him a reassuring pat and took some deep breaths to calm my horse, and myself. We continued around the cliff side, then the trail headed down an overhang that looked to horse and rider as if we were going to end up dropping eighty feet into the river. Just at the edge, the trail took a ninety-degree turn along the bank and finally ended up in open terrain.

Cole said, "Pat, didn't you train your horse to stay on a trail? I thought you two were going to end up falling into the river back there."

"For a couple of seconds, I thought so too. What happened to the *easy-going* trail you told me about?"

"It was easy for these horses; maybe not for an *Arab*," he teased. Cole's mother owned an Arabian horse and on the surface, he was like the rest of the westerners in that he professed to dislike the breed. However, I'd seen him talking and patting my horse when he thought no one was looking. He later admitted to me that Razan was a good horse, "For an *Arab*," he qualified, intending humor.

Rand split the group into thirds, taking turns loping over the trail that wound around sagebrush, cacti and rocks. When we reached a cleared area to rest the horses, Rand said, "If you look to your right, that's what's called "Holy City". Use your imagination and you will see church steeples and temple domes on the crest of those bluffs."

The boys walked off the trail a ways to relieve themselves. I also thought it would be a good place for a pee break and found a large boulder to hide behind on the other side of the trail. Just as I was pulling up my jeans, I heard a car horn beep. I turned around and there was the highway, just on the other side of the river, no more than a couple hundred feet away. People were waving and horns were tooting, at me.

"I wonder if Chief would approve of you exhibiting your wares like that?" Cole joked when I returned to the group.

"I can only hope no one knows where I work," I responded a little embarrassed.

On the return trip, we crossed the river before getting to the narrow cliff trail. "The water's mostly belly deep," Rand told the guests. "If you follow me, swimming will be minimal. If you do not follow me, you and your horse may get caught in the current and be swept down the Shoshone."

I didn't improvise and had my horse follow Rand's horse exactly where he stepped. We climbed the bank on the other side without incident. "Good boy," I said as I patted Razan.

****

Everyone participated in the afternoon's Guest Rodeo in the ranch's rodeo arena. Chief began the rodeo with an equitation class, judging guests' riding ability and improvement. There was an "eleven years and under class", and an "over twelve class". The fun, competitive game events were next. Some required riding horses, like barrel racing and musical chairs (hay bales); while others were done on foot, i.e. roping a fake-steer head. Winners were acknowledged during the evening's talent show.

A guest and longtime friend of Glenn's, named Dave, suggested a wrangler race called an "egg in the mouth" race. I'd entered in gymkhanas (game shows on horseback) as a kid in Maine and thought I knew of every horse game or race invented, but I'd never heard of that race. I wondered what it was! Chief selected six older, non-competitive horses, wrote each name on a piece of paper and the wranglers drew names. I drew Guy, an aging Arab/Appy.

Wranglers had to ride in the saddle that was already on the horse we'd selected—as is, no adjusting stirrups. Facing the gate, on the word "GO" we had to turn and race to the other end of the rodeo arena with a raw egg held in our mouth. Whoever got the other end first, with their egg still in their mouth, in its unbroken shell, won.

Cole won riding Chance, Rand came in second on Happy, Sean got third with Jaws, I came in fourth, Grady dropped his egg on the ground, and Petre's egg broke in his mouth. The guests cheered and loved it. All the wranglers, except Grady, laughed also. He was so angry that later, during a fit of cursing and swearing, he put his fist through the glass in the door window of the saddle shed. I could only hope that he would clean up his language and learn to control his temper before becoming a Mormon minister.

****

After the usual and scrumptious Saturday night prime-rib dinner with mashed potatoes, gravy, string beans, carrots, homemade rolls, and hot fudge sundaes, everyone adjourned to the lodge living room for the talent show.

Whenever 40 guests plus 20 employees get together, there is bound to be unlimited talent. Sometimes I folded paper, origami style, into novelty items to entertain the guests. Other times, I was the mistress of ceremonies. The wrangler boys put on funny skits. The kitchen and cabin staff dressed up like cowgirls and sang country music. Sean, Petre and Fred played guitars and sang western songs. Grady blew up balloons, twisted them into animal shapes, and gave them to the kids. Guests sang, recited poems they'd written, did skits, and told jokes. Guests winning rodeo events received awards and Glenn congratulated all for their participation and sportsmanship. It was a wonderful last evening and end of a great week for the guests.

CHAPTER 17

After a Sunday breakfast of homemade Danish sweet rolls, juice and coffee, Debby, Ann and I saddled up to go for a horse ride before the heat of the day descended. It was July and mid-day to evening was sometimes too hot to ride comfortably, or thundershowers popped up unexpectedly. The air was cool this morning and the horses were feeling fine. Debby was astride Fiddler and Ann was on her favorite mare, MaryJane.

Ann liked Razan and looked at him with interest, commenting to me, "I understand you rode Razan up to Table Mountain. How was his breathing at that altitude?"

"Pretty good," I replied, "his lungs are conditioned now. He got a little nervous on the way up riding behind the other horses but did well leading the group coming back."

Debby said, "He looks like he's adjusted well."

"It helps that he has a friend now, a horse he can boss around so he's not the lowest horse in the pecking order. His friend is Boots. Glenn bought him last week. He's probably old, as he has some arthritic stiffness going on in his front knees. But Razan doesn't care, he likes him anyway. Every time I get through riding Razan, he first does a complete rollover in the small corral to scratch and clean his sweaty skin. Then he hunts for his friend among the other horses and chases him around a bit. Satisfied with his dominance, he drinks from the creek, then hangs out with Boots until they are fed or run out to pasture. It's funny to watch his routine. He's a happy horse."

We had decided to explore the area where Glenn had said Jeremiah Johnson's cabin stood. The trail was only slightly inclined and easy to cover at a brisk trot for the first few miles. Even when the trail got steeper, it was no longer intimidating to me. Everything being relative, I'd already ridden steep and dangerous, so this seemed effortless. The forest was quiet this morning. All big game animals had long gone to the high country to find refuge from the heat. Only coyotes stayed, feasting on the still plentiful hare and rodent population.

Coming to the fork in the trail, we followed the west branch for another mile then dismounted at a clearing where the fir and pine trees looked smaller. We led our horses around until finding the remains of a cabin. Its roof was gone and only two log sides were still standing but it definitely had been someone's cabin. Whether it was Jeremiah Johnson's or not, who knows. Glenn swears that it was.

As we descended the forest trail back toward the ranch, I noticed thunderclouds coming in. We hurried the best we could down the rough trail. About a mile from the ranch, in open terrain, it started pouring rain. Lightening burst from the skies and thunderclaps followed.

I said, "Riding out in the open like this is risky, but I don't know any better trail to take and there is no cover that I can see." I donned my rain slicker, which I'd always tied on back of my saddle, and we kept plodding on toward the ranch amidst the rain, thunder, and lightening. We returned to the corrals safely although Ann and Debby were rain-soaked and cold.

****

We must have been destined for adventure as we planned to go tubing down a creek next Tuesday afternoon. Ann and Debby had tried tubing down Green Creek but it was too shallow and their butts hit too many rocks. Debby had jogged in the area of a creek, about 10 miles west of the ranch, and it looked to her like it would be deep enough to be great tubing. I was game. I'd never tried tubing and it sounded fun to me.

Debby got truck tubes from a garage in Cody, inflated them, and tied them down in the bed of her Chevy S-10. We had to take two vehicles so I drove my car, following Ann and Debby. We stopped at the first bridge on the creek and I parked my car. This way we would have a ride back up stream to Debby's truck once we had "tubed" down the creek. That turned out to be a *very* good plan as it eliminated our walking—unknowingly, in grizzly country.

We put our tubes in the creek about 3-4 miles up from my car, figuring that was far enough to tube for their first time. Luckily, we had worn shorts, T-shirts, and sneakers because at times we scraped against bushes and tree branches hanging over the water's edge and had to push away with our feet. But what fun we had floating downstream on such a lovely warm day, no noise, only us and our tubes, we thought.

About a half-hour had passed when Debby said, "I think the next bridge is where your car is parked, Pat."

I glanced her way and said, "Holy Crap! There's a bear over there on the bank behind you; and I think it's a grizzly."

"What do we do, now?" Ann, always the calm one, said in a whisper. As if the bear cared how loud we spoke.

"I don't know about you, but I'm not stopping to say *howdy*," Debby replied as she began paddling furiously with her hands and kicking her feet to make the tube go faster.

I said, "Let's just keep going downstream and maybe it'll stay where it is." Luckily we were in pretty swift current and we swept right by. Was I scared? You bet... I was petrified! I kept looking behind me to see if the bear was coming after us. I hoped it was hungrier for fish than for females.

In complete silence, we continued tubing until we came to the bridge where I'd parked my car. We stopped at the edge of the creek and elected Debby, the runner, to scout out the road to see if Mr. or Mrs. Bear was around.

"All clear," Debby hollered. We ran to my car and jumped in, leaving the tubes behind.

"Okay, now I hope we don't meet up with that bear on this dirt road because I don't know what it will do, and there is not room to turn my car around if it charges," I said.

We weren't exactly city girls and we knew about bears. However, this was a grizzly and none of us knew anything about grizzly behavior. We only hoped we would not see it again. As luck would have it, we saw the bear again about half way to Debby's truck. However, it was on the other side of the creek moving away. The bear was gone by the time we drove both vehicles back to the main road. We returned to the ranch safe, but still shaken.

We hadn't asked anyone about tubing at that creek as it didn't seem necessary at the time. Later, we learned the name of the creek was Grizzly Creek and it was a prime location for grizzly bears. Our ignorance and brashness could have cost us our lives. As it turned out, we got a well-deserved dressing down by Alice when she found out.

"Don't *ever* take off on your own again without telling me where you're going," Alice said. "You girls don't know this area and we're responsible for you while you live here and work for us." Her point was well taken and remembered.

CHAPTER 18

I was ready for a good night's sleep, hoping I wouldn't dream of being chased by grizzly bears. Entering my cabin, I flicked on the lights, started undressing and got a weird feeling of being watched. I slowly looked around... then screamed.

There was a cowboy boot sticking out from someone (or something) sitting on my toilet. After careful investigation, with my flashlight in my hand for protection, I found the intruder was the ranch's stuffed, cowboy mannequin mascot. About that time, I heard peals of laughing outside and knew I'd been the brunt of another joke.

I couldn't blame Rand this time as he was gone on a pack trip until Friday. I stormed out the door and Fred was rolling around on the ground in a fit of laughter. I went over and kicked him in the butt, saying a few choice cuss words to him. Petre, Ann, Marla, and Sean sat on the ladies' bunkhouse steps chuckling. I brought the cowboy mannequin outside with me to sit where we all had a good laugh and a beer.

Chief told each wrangler that he or she would get a chance to work on a pack trip at least once during the summer. This week was Rand's turn. To make up for the one missing wrangler each week for the next few weeks, Chief hired a new wrangler. "New" being the operative word.

Matt was the son of longtime guests and friends of Glenn and Alice. He was from the Midwest and had the desire to become a mountain wrangler during fall hunting pack trips. He was to apprentice at the ranch for the rest of the summer. However, he had never been around horses.

Chief said to teach Matt everything he needed to know. So we tried. I found it difficult training someone who knew nothing about basic horsemanship, saddling, riding, or guiding. The first day I inspected his horse after he'd tacked it up and he'd put the bridle on the horse, with the bit *outside* the mouth, *under* the jaw. Matt was a real nice young man but he had a lot to learn.

He claimed Ace as his wrangle horse and learned how to saddle and bridle him correctly. As the newest wrangler, he had to wrangle every day until Rand returned. By the end of the summer, I had to give him his due; he'd persevered and eventually made a fine wrangler.

****

Over the weeks, several guests suggested some "hands-on" lessons in horsemanship. The ranch schedule was full and all wranglers usually busy, so there never seemed to be time enough. Now with an extra wrangler around, Chief asked us about teaching an hour-long class. No one volunteered.

He said, "How about you, Pat. You can teach them, can't you?"

"I can do something after lunch on Mondays if another wrangler will help me and demonstrate while I talk." It would cut into my free time, but I reckoned it's only an hour. The other wranglers agreed to take turns helping me. We'd give guests the option of the Three Hour Ride or Horse Lessons in the rodeo corral.

I planned to teach guests useful horse knowledge rather than concentrate on riding heels down, elbows in, etc. I began by describing the use of the bridle and bit, stressing that the bit was not a brake mechanism; it was a communication tool and to use it gently. Sean demonstrated how to saddle a horse while I explained the use of breast collars, stirrups, saddle blankets, and cinching—not too tight, not too loose.

I said to the guests, "You can help us by observing a few things yourself. For instance, if you find yourself riding on your horse's neck, or your saddle is slipping to one side, please ask a wrangler to help you. Your saddle cinch needs to be tightened—and please let us decide that, not you—or your saddle may not fit your horse properly and we'll change it as soon as we can.

"Another thing to notice is saddle blankets. They sometimes slip. If this happens to you or you see it happening to someone riding in front of you, please tell the nearest wrangler. It's simple to correct, but dangerous if they slip out from under the saddle."

I told the guests about horse language, how to tell what horses were thinking. "This comes in very handy preventing accidents or mishaps, like being kicked, bitten, or bucked off.

"Watch their ears. They are signaling devices. If they lay them flat back, look out. They are planning to bite the horse in front of them or kick the horse behind them. Either way, take up your reins, nudge him in his sides, and move him out of the way.

"If a horse is happy, his ears are forward. If he's questioning something, one ear will be forward, the other halfway back or almost pointing at what he is asking about. If they are both partway back, he may be nervous, if his body is also tense; or he may be lazy, if his body and ears are relaxed. Don't worry about halfway back, only flat back."

"Any questions?"

"Yes," said one female guest, "why did Glenn tell us not to let our horses eat grass while we're riding?"

"Good question," I replied. "It's a matter of dominance. With a horse, there is never an equal, not between horses, not between horse and rider. One is always the boss. We would rather *you* be the boss, things will go better for you and the rest of the riders.

"That doesn't mean you tell your horse where he should step. You don't have to guide him as he knows these trails and how to best negotiate them much better than you. So let him do his job. What I'm talking about is getting his respect so he will pay attention, for instance, if you need him to move out of the way quickly. And you don't have to beat him or abuse him to get his attention.

"If you have let him graze anytime he wants to or lag behind however slow he wants to go, he will not respect your commands. He will think he's the boss, and he intends to stay that way.

"The simplest way for you to show your horse that you are the boss, right from the start— today, Monday—is to *not* let him eat grass while you are riding. You can easily control that by keeping the reins short enough so that he can't put his head down to graze. That simple act alone will show him that *you* are the boss and *you* decide what he is to do, not him. And don't give in, even once, or you'll lose your dominance.

"Another reason for not letting your horse graze, is safety. If he's stopped to eat, all horses behind him in line have to stop and they might be at a place on the trail where it's dangerous for them to stop. So try not to have this happen. Keep them moving not eating."

I wound down my talk by having Sean name and show the major parts of a horse's body and explain what their functions are.

Glenn had walked down to the rodeo arena where I was giving my talk. When I'd finished and we were heading back to the corrals, he said, "Good job, I think that's what they wanted to learn. We'll do that again next week."

CHAPTER 19

Guests came and went weekly, their names disappearing when the next group arrived. However, some left an impression. Amelia was such a guest. She came from Connecticut with her sister to ride, not raft down the Shoshone, or sightsee in Yellowstone. She rode every day, morning and afternoon. On Friday, she and I did the Eagle Cliffs ride. I rode Crystal again and Amelia was astride long-legged Rowdy.

We had a lot in common and chatted as we rode. We both skied and were businesswomen in our real, other lives. We neared the halfway point up the ledges when I suddenly realized that Amelia had become quiet.

I looked over my shoulder to make sure she was still behind me and said, "Are you okay? You're awfully quiet all of a sudden."

"I have a problem with vertigo, but I'm trying to live with it and I'm alright," she replied.

"Let me know if you get sick, dizzy, or need to stop," I said, knowing that there was no real good place to stop on these ledges. I wished Amelia had said something about her phobia earlier; I could have found an easier trail to test her fortitude.

Although I greatly respected Amelia's desire to overcome her phobia, Eagle Cliffs trail was definitely *not* the trail one should ride if one has vertigo.

****

Judge J was another memorable guest. He was a retired New York Supreme Court Judge in his late 70's and had been a guest at Rimrock for the past 25 years. He sometimes repeated questions when meeting people, but he always remembered everyone's name. I was impressed. That was more than I could do at my younger age.

Alice asked me to guide him on a solo ride around the ranch advising me that the judge couldn't see too well.

"You'll need to tell him if he needs to duck under limbs or any other problem that he might need to prepare for while riding. He always rides Hugo, who is the best trail horse here on the ranch, but Hugo won't necessarily look out for the Judge. You'll have to do that."

Whereas Judge J was getting frail, four male wranglers helped him mount; but once astride, he was fairly, well balanced. I guided him across Canyon Creek and immediately Judge J asked me to turn left and take a trail through the cottonwoods that followed along the creek. This was a new one to me and I gladly guided him on the newly discovered trail. We rode around the introductory loop, with a few new variations, as requested by Judge J. We returned to the ranch with no mishaps. He was a wise and delightful gentleman.

****

A guest had been observing the boys trying, unsuccessfully for a half-hour, to put shoes on Nemo's hind feet. They couldn't even get near his hind quarters without the horse kicking out. The guest asked Glenn if he could show them a training technique new to the West but growing in popularity around the country. The method was called "round penning". He said that his demonstration might be of interest to some of the other guests and wranglers and he'd do it after lunch.

I had heard of round-pen training and was very anxious to see it demonstrated. I was very interested in any kind of horse training, hoping to have some time to work with the ranch's wild mustang colt and fillies purchased from the Bureau of Land Management last spring.

Chief also showed up at the small corral. All cowboys used to, and most still did, train a horse by "breaking" it. They'd rope the horse, force a halter onto it and hog-tie it if it moved too much. This meant snubbing its nose close to a post and tying up one leg so it couldn't move. They'd throw on a blanket, a saddle, and mount up while someone else untied it. And away they'd go. The scared horse bucked around the corral until it got so tired it couldn't buck any more. That may have shown the horse that the cowboy was dominant, but it sure didn't teach the horse to trust. Therefore, horses were not safe for novices to ride until they were nearing seven years old. This new technique would be interesting.

The guest, Rodney, first took Nemo's halter off, then made him move around by stepping toward him every time he stopped and making a clicking sound with his mouth. Then Rodney stepped it up a notch and forced Nemo to trot round the pen, making the clicking sound and tossing the end of a lariat close to the horse's rear if he slowed. At times, Rodney would step toward the front of the horse, facing it, holding his near-arm out straight shaking the rope, while pointing with his other arm to the opposite direction. The horse would turn and trot in the other direction.

After about ten minutes, Nemo stopped and faced Rodney, making a chewing movement with his mouth, looking him right in the eye. Rodney walked up to the horse, patted him on the forehead, neck, and front quarters, then walked toward the center of the pen clicking as he went. Nemo followed. Rodney patted him all over this time, including his hindquarters and his hind legs. The horse fidgeted a bit and Rodney sent him off at a trot again.

A few more times around and Nemo stopped and faced Rodney again. Once more he went through his patting routine then reached for Nemo's hind leg. Nemo stood still. Rodney picked it up and Nemo's ears flicked back but he didn't move. Rodney crossed to the other side, patted the horse and reached to pick up the off rear leg. Nemo kicked out and got sent around the pen a few times more at a canter.

The next time Nemo stopped. Rodney picked up each hoof, cleaned it out, and set it back down. The horse stood at ease and never moved.

The guests clapped. Chief and the boys were impressed. After putting Nemo back in the shoeing area, they went to talk to Rodney more about this method. I understood; it was all about dominance. Young and unruly horses were safer to work with from the ground. This was a safe and effective way of using the horse's natural herd instinct of acquiescing to the dominant animal, in this case, Rodney. Good job Rodney.

I figured I would try this method on the young wild horses. They were still in a pasture just off the driveway and not put out with the main herd. I could work with them evenings right after supper.

I worked with each of the three yearling fillies first. I got them to the round pen with the assistance of another wrangler. Usually Petre was willing to help. At first I just made them move at a walk, then pushed them to a trot, changing directions periodically. These fillies were used to acquiescing as youngsters always acknowledge older horses as dominant. They quickly accepted me as their "alpha" leader.

All I could do to these yearlings was teach them to lead, and stand tied while I brushed, groomed and picked up their feet. I accomplished this with alacrity.

Next, I wanted to work with Shiloh, a two and a half-year-old pinto. His disposition was friendly and he showed no fear of humans. He accepted my dominance with surprising speed. I led him everywhere within walking distance on the ranch.

Over the next few weeks, I proceeded to put a bridle on him and got him to accept a bit in his mouth. I sacked him out with a blanket, rain slicker, and anything else I could find that might spook him. Shiloh was unfazed.

I found a lightweight ladies' saddle, strapped it on him, and let him run and buck in the round pen. When he'd gotten used to it, I stepped up to him, quietly mounted, sat there a minute patting him, and got off. For the next couple of times that was all I did, sitting on his back longer each time. Soon I was riding him around the pen at a walk. He was not old enough or big enough yet to train him on the trail. I hoped whoever worked with him in the next year(s) would be as gentle with him. Shiloh would never need to be "broken", just trained.

****

Glenn said he had an unusually large pack trip going over Eagle Pass into Yellowstone soon, with a group from New York City. He asked me to go along as an extra wrangler and public relations person. Apparently the group leader, Sandy, was apt to be finical and fussy and Glenn seemed to think I

95

could handle her attitude! I had my doubts, but agreed to go along as I'd heard that the trip over Eagle Pass was spectacular. I'd also be interested in seeing Yellowstone Park's new forest growth after the big fires of a few years past.

I hoped to hear from Dustin before I left on a pack trip for a week or more, or our paths might not cross again all summer.

CHAPTER 20

Friday evening, Glenn told me that my pack trip would be leaving on Sunday. Luckily, Dustin called Saturday evening. He chuckled when I told him I was leaving tomorrow to pack over Eagle Pass into Yellowstone.

"I've just returned from that area and I'm going back out Monday. We'll follow Clear Creek to Yellowstone Lake, down the Yellowstone River to Mountain Creek, then back through Eagle Pass. We'll be camped at Eagle Creek Meadow Thursday night and pack out Friday."

"I don't know our exact route or timing," I replied, "only that we're staying at Eagle Creek Meadow the first and the last nights out. We leave Sunday and are supposed to be back Friday. Wow, that puts us there on Thursday night, also. Can we all camp there at the same time?"

"No problem. The meadow is at least three miles long and there are three different camping spots spread throughout the valley."

"It would be cool if we spent the night in the same valley. I'd really like to see you again."

"It wouldn't be cool if we spent the night together, Hon, it would be more like "hot". Maybe we can take a pack trip together at the end of the season."

"I'd like that. Guess we'll just have to wait and see what happens."

We said our good-byes, hoping to meet up on the trail.

I made ready for the trek tomorrow packing a duffel bag with warm clothes, i.e. heavy sweater, wool socks, and long underwear. I'd wear chaps, light jacket, and gloves; tie a heavy jacket and slicker onto my saddle; and put a scarf, extra socks and another pair of gloves in my saddlebag. I'd ridden over the Continental Divide twice before and knew that it could rain or snow real quick in high elevation and I wanted to be neither wet nor cold.

Glenn had told me to put my horse in the local pasture with the young mustangs while I was gone.

"Raisin doesn't have a brand on him like the rest of our horses," Glenn said, "and he looks too nice down in the highway pastures. He's also too friendly and a traveler might be tempted to load him up and take him away."

At least I knew my horse would be safe near the ranch. I also asked Cole to check on Razan occasionally.

There were seven guests from New York City, all friends or relatives, and one lady, Annette from Rhode Island, going on the pack trip. Glenn had given Annette a free trip because she'd broken her wrist while walking down Rampart Pass on a previous pack trip and never complained or asked for special treatment. She was a good sport and Glenn appreciated the cowgirl in her. I had met Annette on my first pack trip to Jackson Hole. It would be nice to see her again.

Five black packhorses, Jerry's guide horse Cowtown, and four riding horses were already in corrals at the Eagle Creek trailhead. They could stay there from one trek to another as long as there was only a couple of days in between treks. It was up to the trail guides to make sure the horses were watered and fed daily.

Early Sunday morning, Jerry and Travis loaded Nemo, Earl, Beauty, Dixie, Sankey, Brownie, Bomber, Badger, Cassie, Cub, and Jubilee into the horse van and took them to the trailhead. The truck carried horse tack, chairs, guest tents and tarps. As soon as they arrived at the trailhead they fed and watered all the animals and then started sorting and packing. It would take three to four hours to get it all done.

Liz and I followed with a truck filled with the food panniers and cooking equipment. Liz was the ranch breakfast cook and substitute pack-trip cook. She was replacing Fred, who had a family wedding to attend in Montana. I was to ride Stubby, Fred's usual mountain horse, and Liz would ride Dixie.

Packing horses was very precise and difficult work. Fortunately, Jerry and Travis had a lot of previous experience and began strapping on the packsaddles. Liz was busy filling panniers with foodstuffs. Cook gear, bedrolls, duffels, and tents were then placed on top of the panniers and covered by tarps tied down with rope. My job was to saddle the riding horses. That meant I had to groom, blanket, saddle and bridle twelve horses, every day. I wanted to be a cowgirl and this was part of it—"So enjoy it," I told myself.

The van carrying the guests arrived and their duffels were prepared for packing. The guests stood around socializing until all packhorses were packed and riding horses, saddled. Annette had immediately come to my aid helping me tack up the last of the riding horses. I appreciated her help, and thanked her profusely.

Jerry assigned a riding horse to each guest. Travis and I fitted their stirrups, giving them a few basic instructions, i.e. do not lag behind, and do not crowd each other on the trail.

Jerry said, "Mount up, let's move out."

CHAPTER 21

From the trailhead, the pack trippers immediately crossed Eagle Creek, with Jerry leading a string of five packhorses and Travis leading a string of four. Liz followed next, then the New York City guests, then Annette. I bought up the rear.

Eagle Creek proved too deep for Sankey, a small but sturdy packhorse, and he lost his footing. He would have been swept down river except that he was tied to the other packhorses and they pulled him across. His pack kept him afloat. Some bedding got wet, however Sankey wasn't upset, he ate grass on the other side while waiting for the rest of us to cross.

That was too much excitement, already, for Cindy, one of the city guests. She refused to cross the river riding Earl.

Jerry yelled, "Pat, grab Earl's reins and lead him across. Cindy, you stay in the saddle and do not move. It's either ride or swim."

Once we were on the trail, things settled down. The trail wound smoothly through the tranquil forest. I even spotted a moose hiding in some swamp brush watching the trekkers. The trail gradually ascended hills, once parched by fire, then descended toward the creek again. At noon, Liz, the guests and

I stopped alongside the creek and ate cold bag lunches while the packhorses and guides kept traveling toward the campsite.

Late afternoon we arrived at Eagle Creek Meadow, also known as Three Mile Meadow. The camp was set up at the third and far campsite. The guests' tents were erected and the cook's tent assembled. Jerry was chopping wood for the fire; Travis was tethering two of the mares, Cassie and Brownie; and the packhorses were grazing unrestrained nearby.

I turned the remaining horses loose to graze after I'd unsaddled them. I placed each saddle, with blankets and bridle, on a long log and covered them all with a tarp in case of rain. Next I collected my duffel and set about putting up my own tent. I was the last one to pick up a bedroll and pillow. Unfortunately, the bedroll was the one that got wet when Sankey fell in the creek. I strung a line near the fire to dry the bedding. It was only partly dry when I put it in my tent that night. I found I was so tired, I slept soundly, wet bedding and all.

Morning brought fog and two young moose playing behind my tent in the tall grasses. I watched them for a while before getting up and telling the others. I found the fire roaring and coffee hot. Pack-trip coffee is not brewed, and definitely not instant. A metal coffeepot filled with water is put onto the open fire. Once boiling, loose coffee grounds are dumped in and the pot was set aside to simmer. After a few minutes, an eggshell is dropped into the coffee to collect the grounds to the bottom of the pot, and the coffee is ready to drink—strong but good.

I had retired early last evening and missed some of the guests' requests and complaints. Jerry said that Sandy and her sister Cindy complained because they found pine needles in their tent. He said, "I think they expected a five star hotel with a chocolate on their pillow. I handed them a dustpan and asked if there was anything else I could help them with.

"They wanted to know where the bathroom was…I showed them the spade and toilet paper and said 'Anywhere you want'. They huffed and went back into their tent. They may start turning brown with constipation if they don't learn how to shit in the woods before we get back on Friday."

The men guests complained about the ground being hard, and the ladies were late for breakfast. Liz held off throwing breakfast in the fire as long as she could, but the outfit was moving over Eagle Pass and everyone needed to get started. The city ladies were roused out of their tent at nine. Breakfast was at seven.

Before continuing up the pass, Jerry decided he had better get a few things straight with the guests.

"I heard a lot of complaining last night and this morning about too dirty, too cold, too hard, etc. The brochures that were sent you said, 'This trip is a progressive trek for six days and five nights, covering fifteen miles each day on horseback over mountains and sleeping in two-person tents on the ground at night.' It was never billed as a plush, easy ride, with hot showers and a feather bed at the end of each day.

"Now, we can turn around and go back to the ranch if that's what you want. But, if we go on over the pass to Yellowstone Park, I don't want to hear any more complaining or bellyaching. You decide, and tell me in the next ten minutes, which way we go."

Everyone was silent.

Finally, the guests held a whispered conference. The consensus was to continue over the pass, and stop complaining.

The Eagle Pass trail climbed steeply through forested switchbacks until just before reaching the summit of near 9600 feet. There the trail crossed open ledges. Looking over the trailside at the terrain dropping a few hundred feet caused most first timers to become anxious. Cindy was petrified. Earl was as cautious and surefooted as a horse could be, but Cindy wasn't mollified. She wanted to get off her horse and walk, but of course, there was no place for her to dismount. The trail was only a couple of feet wide.

Jerry had reached the summit and upon hearing Cindy's crying, tied up Cowtown and his pack string. He walked back, urging the others to find a tree or shrub and tie up at the summit near his horses. I was behind Cindy and unable to pass or dismount to help. Jerry appeared and, just short of threatening Cindy with bodily harm, told her to stop crying, keep her mouth shut, and he'd lead her the rest of the way to the summit.

We all took a badly needed break before descending to Howell Creek and easier riding. Jerry placed Cindy between his pack team and Travis's. I was thankful. Putting up with Cindy's hysterical tantrums was more than I'd bargained for. Riding behind the trekkers was again peaceful and quiet. We were now in Yellowstone Park.

Jerry had planned to camp on the Yellowstone River and fish for the legendary Yellowstone cutthroat trout. However, the guests were only interested in reaching a campsite. Therefore, we stopped to camp a few miles before the river, along Mountain Creek, in an area previously burned in the Yellowstone fires. New green grasses and growths of new pine trees surrounded charred tree trunks on still burnt ground. One life gone, new life begins.

For supper, Liz prepared Italian spaghetti and meatballs with tossed salad, and garlic bread. Tom, Sandy's brother, opened two bottles of merlot wine and shared it with everyone. Tasty cherry tarts cooked over hot embers were dessert.

Annette and I shared a tent that night, as it meant one less tent to put up and take down. Early morning we heard rustling outside. Something was nuzzling our tent. We'd all been warned that this was grizzly country and we should never have any food or gum in our tent—we didn't, but the rustling continued. Neither of us dared unzip the tent flap and look out. We waited silently until we heard Jerry and Liz talking in the cook tent. The rustling turned out to be our horses grazing around our tent.

However, later that morning, following the Yellowstone, Jerry pointed out a female grizzly and her cub climbing the hillside across the river. When we stopped for lunch Travis noticed fresh grizzly prints in the sand and nearby were large grizzly scat piles that were almost the size of a horse manure pile. These were constant reminders of the presence of grizzlies. Jerry told us that the grizzly numbers had increased substantially and are now under consideration to be removed from the Endangered Species List. Every night our food supplies were hoisted 10' high and hung between trees, out of grizzly reach.

We followed the river valley to a point near the confluence of the Thorofare and Yellowstone Rivers, then rode east to the Thorofare Ranger Station. The log cabin, barn, and corrals were historic structures nestled next to a hillside. No one was there. Such peace, quiet and solitude are hard to find nowadays. I immediately fell in love with the area.

Jerry said, "This territory around the ranger station is considered the most remote place in the continental United States. The region is called the Thorofare because it's wide and easy to travel. For centuries, Indians and fur trappers used this route. Mountain man Jim Bridger named nearby Bridger Lake. This valley is approximately fourteen miles long and three miles wide and remains just as wild and free as it was 200 years ago. We Americans are fortunate to have such a designated wilderness area as this."

I wondered if the city slickers appreciated being here.

We set up early camp along the Thorofare River just beyond the ranger station. What a spectacular place to camp, I thought. *If* Dustin and I ever get to go packing, this is where I would like to go.

Camp was all set up by mid-afternoon. The sun was shining brightly and blue skies were abundant. There was plenty of time to take a hike and explore, or take a swim in the peaceful, sublime river. The guests chose to relax in the folding camp chairs and read. Jerry was replacing shoes on a couple of his horses. Travis was digging a pit for Liz to cook a roast in the ground for tonight's supper. I wanted to test the water to feel how cold it was as I'd like to swim and wash my hair if it wasn't *too* cold.

Annette joined me at the water's edge, both of us wore shorts and had towels draped over our shoulders. I stepped in first, knee deep off a rock, and immediately stepped out. "I can't believe it's that cold," I said. I tried it again in a shallow place by the edge of the river. "This water is colder than the Atlantic Ocean along the Maine coast."

We finally went to Liz for a cooking pan, which we used to pour the river water over our hair before and after lathering with shampoo. "Brrrrrrr," said Annette, "this is as far as I'm getting into this ice water."

"Me too, I'll just wash strategic places with a soapy cloth and call it good until I get back to the ranch to shower."

We met Travis on our way to our tent and he laughed at our tale of woe. "Of course the river's cold; it's snowmelt directly from those mountain tops over there." He pointed northeast to snowcapped peaks no more than five miles away. "Heat water over the fire and use a wash pan like the rest of us mountain men do."

Annette and I felt a little foolish at our naiveté, but we were clean anyway.

Twenty horses, eighty hooves, thundering down the valley woke me the next morning. Travis was behind them driving them to the river to drink before being packed and tacked up for the day's ride. I slipped into my jeans and boots, strapped on my chaps and put on my jacket, gloves and hat. Mornings were beautiful but chilly here in the valley. I got the horses' grain cubes from the cook tent and emptied them into two large ground-buckets. This would entice the horses to stay around until I slipped halters onto them and tied them to trees.

The aroma of hotcakes, eggs and bacon frying permeated the air drawing guests, both men and women, from their tents. Jerry had told them that today's trek would be easy and they were actually looking forward to riding. The group rode south and west around Bridger Lake, then followed the Yellowstone River north to Mountain Creek. The ride up the valley was quiet and effortless. The guests enjoyed it, and pleasing them was important. I looked forward to climbing Eagle Pass again.

We camped at the confluence of Mountain and Howell Creek, not far from where we had camped two nights ago. Apparently, it had just dawned on the guests that we had been riding on the same trail, for the last ten miles, that we had ridden coming down from Eagle Pass.

In a state of panic, Cindy asked Jerry, "Do we have to go over that same pass again?"

"Yep," he replied.

"Can't we go home another way?"

"Nope."

"Is there any way I can get home without riding Earl?"

"Yep, you can walk, we'll lead Earl."

"Can you call a helicopter to come get me?"

"Nope, not unless you break an arm, or leg, or have a heart attack. You'd be wasting their valuable time and I won't do it."

"I think I'm going to be sick."

"We'll help you the best we can. Have a little faith in us. We've been packing over mountain passes for quite a few years and we've never lost a guest yet. Horses, yes; guests, no."

Just before dawn the next morning, the camp awoke suddenly to: *rattle, bang, clatter, clang.*

"Oh no, I don't even want to think about what that was about," I whispered to Annette. "I'm staying inside this tent until sunup or until I hear familiar voices outside."

When the sun surfaced, Jerry told us that there had been a bear rummaging around in the cook's tent. "Ordinarily I would have shot over its head to scare it off, but guns are illegal in Yellowstone Park. They want us to use pepper spray," he said rolling his eyes. "I carry a 44- magnum in my pack but I'd use it only if it was a life threatening situation. I think it was a black bear not a grizzly and it was just being nosey not threatening, so I rattled a few pans to scare it off."

Well now, this day had started out exhilarating. I wondered what excitement Eagle Pass would bring.

Jerry had, somewhat, convinced Cindy that it was safer to ride Earl across the open ledges of Eagle Pass and down the switchbacks, than for her to try to walk it herself. While everyone stopped at the top for a breather, he took me aside.

"Pat, will you lead Cindy from your horse? Keep her close and talk to her constantly to keep her mind off the steep terrain. Are you comfortable doing this?"

"Sure, I'll turn around and talk her through it. I'm riding Stubby and he's negotiated steep trails for the past five years, according to Fred, so I shouldn't have to pay attention to him. We'll be okay."

And we were okay. I had Cindy look to my left, up the mountain, instead of ahead or down the fall line. When we reached the meadows below, she said to me, "Thank you so much, I owe you, big-time."

We rode the length of the Eagle Creek Meadow, stopping at the last campsite, as was customary among packers. This was done as a courtesy so if another outfitter used the valley to camp at the same time, they wouldn't have to pass through a herd of horses grazing free on the tall, meadow grasses.

Jerry knew that Dustin might be camping in the same meadow that night so he told Travis to tether three mares instead of two. If our horses strayed throughout the long meadow, and they might with another herd around, he, Travis, and I might have a difficult time rounding them up. Generally, with one or two mares staked near the campsite, at least one mare would be in heat. That meant some of the geldings would be sure to stay close, and where a group of horses remained, the whole herd would likely stay nearby. He also tied a bell around the necks of the hard to catch horses, Nemo and Bomber.

I put up my tent on the far outskirts of camp and asked Annette if she'd mind sleeping in her own tent that night, "Just in case I have company".

With a sly grin, Annette said, "I don't mind as long as you help me put it up and take it down in the morning. *And* keep the noise to a minimum if you and Dustin get together!"

To my delight, Dustin came walking into our campsite that evening. He already knew Jerry and Travis; I introduced him to Annette, and to Sandy's city group. We all sat around the campfire and chatted for a while then drifted off to our tents.

There was not much chatter between Dustin and I once we got to my tent. For one, there was little to no privacy; and two, we had more urgent matters that needed taking care of.

Dustin awoke before dawn, "Listen," he said.

"I don't hear anything," I replied.

"That's the problem, no noise. No snorting, blowing, whinnying, no bells tinkling, no hooves stamping or rustling of grasses. Too quiet. I'm going to awaken Jerry and see what's up."

Unfortunately, Rimrock's horses did not stay close that night.

At daybreak, Dustin, Jerry and Travis saddled the three lone mares and set off to find the others. Soon Travis came back with a few of the blacks. "Pat, you need to saddle a horse and come help. Our horses are all intermixed with Dustin's and we need to separate them and bring ours back. Ebony hasn't been ridden for a long time, but I think he's saddle broke. Liz and Annette, can you halter the other four so they don't follow us?"

I threw a saddle on Ebony. He was full of nervous energy and wanted to go. I had to lead him to a tree stump to mount up; he was half Percheron and over sixteen hands. Ebony crow-hopped across the campsite before finally settling down to a consistent trot. I followed a grinning Travis.

"Hey cowgirl, I didn't know you could ride that well. Good job staying on." Travis said as we rode up the meadow looking for any stray horses along the way.

"I didn't just come off the city streets, you know; I *can* ride. But, it's a good thing he stopped bucking when he did. I don't think I could have stayed on much longer."

We spotted Jerry and Dustin each attempting to cut out their own horses from the combined group of nearly thirty horses. Dustin's wrangler joined him, and with Travis and my help, the cutting was more successful. Travis roped Elvira, who was a half sister to Ebony, handed the lariat to me and said, "Why don't you lead her back to the campsite; start slowly. Jerry is roping Cowtown, who's another dominant horse, and will lead him back, too. I'll round up the rest and hopefully they'll follow you guys."

They did. Crisis over.

Even with the extra ride down the meadow, it was still early so Jerry sent me back to Dustin's camp to get Brownie. I saddled Stubby this time and really enjoyed the morning ride alone. I spotted a bull moose at the far edge of the meadow and jumped two mule deer out of a thicket of brush.

Dustin greeted me as I approached his camp.

"Would you like some breakfast before you ride back across the meadow, again? It's all ready."

"Love some."

I was hungry and quickly devoured scrambled eggs with sausage and homefries. "I'd better be headed back or Jerry will be wondering if I got ambushed by moose or something."

Dustin held Stubby while I mounted and handed Brownie's reins to me. He put his hand on my leg and reached up to kiss me. "Well cowgirl, it was a lovely night. Morning came way too soon. I'll call you in between trips, okay? Take care."

"You too, glad we could meet up here in the meadow, nice place. See ya…soon I hope."

Back at my campsite, the blacks had their packtrees strapped on, waiting the panniers and camp gear. I caught the remaining saddle horses and started grooming. Annette came over to help. "Nice guy, this Dustin cowboy, huh?"

"Yeah, I think so. Wish I could pack with him for a while."

"Maybe next summer," Annette said with a wink.

"Maybe, we'll see."

The return trek was quiet and uneventful. Sankey managed to stay upright traversing Eagle Creek and even the guests were serene and seemed melancholy upon reaching the trailhead.

Sandy actually told me, "We've had the experience of our lifetime." She didn't clarify if it was good or bad. I didn't ask. Rimrock's van was waiting to take the guests back to their motel in Cody. Annette and I said our good-byes and promised to keep in touch.

While I piled the saddles, breast collars, blankets, and bridles into the back of the waiting pickup Petre had driven to the trailhead, Liz and Petre loaded the panniers and the five extra tents. Liz and I rode back to the ranch with Petre. Jerry and Travis would follow with five of the horses loaded in the horse van once they got the horses that were to remain at the corrals, watered and fed.

They had a small pack trip leaving Sunday, a group of five guests. Petre would replace Travis as wrangler, as he had to get ready to go back to college. Fred would return as pack cook.

CHAPTER 22

At the ranch, I returned each saddle to its numbered spot in the saddle shed, then almost ran to the showers. I couldn't remember when I'd been this dirty for this long. Ah, hot running water at last.

My second duty was to see how my horse had fared while I'd been gone. Razan trotted over to me in response to my whistle; so did the young mustangs. Razan was bigger, older, and in charge. He'd gained a little weight from lack of exercise and grazing on irrigated pasture grass. I thought he looked good. I'd leave him there until I talked with Chief about where to put him.

When I checked into the lodge for mail, I found a message from the Horsin' Around Transport Company. They would be in the Cody area Thursday and could pick my horse up to take him back to Maine. I was to call them immediately. I'd also have to schedule a vet check before Thursday.

Returning after packing out for a week was like having jet lag and culture shock all at once. I found it difficult to get back up to speed. To make matters worse, things were changing at the ranch, much to my chagrin. Travis and Cole left to find a house to rent for the four of them, Travis, Sean, Cole, and Rand, in Bozeman while they attended Montana State University. Grady had gone back to Utah last week. There was a new wrangler, Bill, an older cowboy who would help take up the slack of the boys leaving early. He would remain, as would Mike, to work as wrangler through hunting season. Petre and I would stay through August.

After I sent Razan back to Maine with the horse transport company, I spent time working with the mustangs evenings but I missed having my own horse to ride on my days off. I also missed Dustin. He was still packing and wouldn't have any free time until Labor Day Weekend. We'd made plans to get together then. However this Sunday I was off, with nothing to do.

Petre and I had previously talked about making a sojourn through Yellowstone Park to Jackson Hole and this Sunday would be our last chance to go. I had never been into Jackson and Petre wanted to continue south to Big Piney to visit a cattle ranch where he'd worked the previous summer.

We didn't realize what a long trip we were making in just one day. We left before breakfast and encountered snow squalls as I drove through the East Entrance of the Park and carefully over Sylvan Pass. On the other side of the pass, a herd of buffalo crowded the highway along Yellowstone Lake disrupting traffic. At West Thumb, we switched drivers and Petre drove south past Lewis Lake and out Yellowstone's South Entrance into the Grand Teton National Park.

There were no foothills here, which accentuated the Teton Range's dramatic rise. Jackson Lake reflected their rocky cliffs, glaciers, aspen groves and the pine forests. I found something mesmerizing about looking at the majestic snow-capped peaks, hypnotic, like gazing into a fire. The view from the smaller Jenny Lake, nestled at the foot of the Grand Teton, was spectacular. I decided I'd also like to pack through this valley sometime. At this rate, I'd have to spend the rest of my summers packing, to see and experience all I wanted of the west.

Downtown Jackson was inundated with gift shops and art galleries catering to tourists. I decided I preferred the more relaxed atmosphere of Cody. Petre and I snapped pictures of each other under the Elkhorn Archways of Jackson's Town Square, then ate lunch at Bubba's BBQ on West Broadway before proceeding to Big Piney.

Petre hadn't mentioned to me that Big Piney was 90 miles south of Jackson—no one was at the ranch—and another 90 miles to Farson, which was only mid-way through our trip! It was already two o'clock and we'd been traveling six hours. If we didn't get back by seven, in time for introductions, Alice would be very angry.

There was little traffic through Riverton and the Wind River Canyon and we made good time. Through the flat land from Thermopolis to Cody, we exceeded the speed limit by at least 25 mph. We pulled into the ranch parking lot at 6:55 pm. Petre jumped out to get his guitar, while I quickly ran for the lodge.

We made it just in time, puffing and out of breath. We'd been gone twelve hours and the other employees chided us about eloping or thinking we had runaway together. We took the teasing in good humor; we were just glad to be back.

****

Debby left to apprentice polo in Argentina the next week; I wished her the best. Sean and Rand left for college. I had really liked working with the boys: Rand, Sean, Cole, and Travis. I would miss them. They treated me as their equal and with respect.

On the other hand, Bill, the older cowboy, treated me as if I didn't know one end of a horse from the other; he was obnoxious, patronizing, and chauvinistic. When Chief made me the head wrangler after Rand left for college, things just got worse. He spat and said "I'm not taking orders from any *female*."

Chief replied, "You will or you'll find another job."

Bill stayed but his attitude didn't change. Thankfully, the other wranglers worked hard to make up for Bill's disrespect.

I did the best job I could do, given the circumstances. I figured I only had two more weeks here anyway, so I just ignored Bill and his rude, sarcastic comments. I knew it was time to leave while I still had mostly good memories.

****

Dustin called the Friday before Labor Day and he and I made plans to meet at his cabin early the next Sunday morning.

Until then, I had my gear to gather and pack, and good-byes to say. I hugged Glenn and Alice, wished them the best, and hoped to see them again sometime. Glenn told me to take good care of that *Arab*. Alice smiled, thinking of her own Arabian. Petre and I agreed to keep in touch via letters. I would miss the tranquil beauty of Wapiti Valley.

CHAPTER 23

I drove slowly toward Pahaska reflecting on my summer experiences. Spending the next two days with Dustin would likely be my last adventure here in Wyoming.

I had never been to Dustin's cabin but he'd given me driving directions from the Pahaska Tepee Resort located just outside Yellowstone's East Entrance. I took the next left and drove about a half-mile on a dirt road then spotted an A-frame cabin on my right.

Dustin came to meet me from his horse shed and corral area. It looked like he only had three horses in the corral. "Hey, cowgirl, glad you found my place okay."

"Hey, yourself," I replied as I reached up and gave him a kiss on his cheek. "Where are the rest of your horses?"

"I took all but these three to my parents ranch to rest and fatten up before they have to endure hunting trips later this month. I kept this young paint mare here just for you. I think you'll like her; she's a five year old, Half Arab/Half Quarter horse. Name's Reena."

She stood about 14.3 hands and was nicely built, with good legs, soft intelligent eyes, wide forehead, and small ears—very

Arab looking. She also had a strong chest and rump—very Quarter horse. Her color was a deep sorrel with a white strip, four white stockings, and a large white patch on her left shoulder and right rump. Her mane, forelock and tail were black, brown and white. I liked the looks of her. "Is she trained for pack trips?" I asked.

"She's trained, but has never done a pack trip. I didn't want to take her out packing for the first time with guests on board. This will be good experience for her. Her dam is my Mom's mare; we raised her."

"What about climbing the pass, will she be okay?"

"Well, we need to talk about that, Hon. You said you'd like to ride up Eagle Pass and camp near the Thorofare but that's not possible now. It snowed there last week and the trail isn't safe for horses. So if it's okay with you, we'll just stay camped at Three Mile Meadow and explore."

"Fine, by me."

"If you want to throw your gear in the truck bed and park your car over there by the cabin, I think we're about ready to go."

****

We unloaded Dustin's truck and horse trailer at the trailhead and set to work getting the horses ready. He saddled my horse for me. It was nice being waited on for a change.

"Reena has a very soft mouth so I've been riding her with just a headstall and no bit. If you want, I'll put a snaffle on her," he said.

"No, that's fine. I frequently ride my horse with no bit when I'm on the trail."

Dustin's horse was a seasoned gelding who'd been lame most of the summer but was sound again now. He was a big bay

Quarter horse with a white blaze and one white sock, named Cochise.

I helped Dustin finish packing the third horse, Runner. He showed me how to tie the pack with a double diamond hitch. I hoped I didn't have to remember that one.

We crossed the river without incident and wound our way along the trail at a nice steady trot. Reena and I got along just fine, being an Arab (at least part), the mare responded well to soft hands and a gentle touch. We arrived at the meadow early afternoon.

Dustin said, "Let's take the trail on the right and camp at the further end. I want to show you something."

About a mile down the meadow, Dustin pointed out a wrecked airplane in amongst some brush and trees. He said, "A few years ago, someone crashed this plane and for some reason, there it stays. No one ever claimed it or hauled it out of here. Looks a little out of place, don't you think?"

"That's weird," I replied. "What were they poaching and didn't want to get caught?"

"Probably, it's a large wilderness area for wardens to patrol, mostly by horseback. If they have a suspect they're hunting for, then they might use a helicopter or small plane."

We did an easy lope to the end of the meadow, had cold sandwiches for lunch, and set up camp. After the horses were watered and staked out, Dustin asked, "Did you bring some foot gear you can hike in?"

"I've got sneakers with good tread."

"Let's hike part way up that mountain. There's an old mine we can explore," he said as he changed into his hiking boots.

The afternoon was a pleasant 55 degrees and just right for hiking, although I was a little out of breath from the altitude. Once we reached the mine, we surveyed the entire length of the meadow settled in-between nine thousand-foot peaks. All that remained to observe of the old mine was a decrepit shaft, but we did find two obsidian arrowhead tips and a flaking stone left behind from the arrowhead-carving process.

"Removing antique items is prohibited by the Antiquities Act," Dustin told me, so we stuck the arrowheads and stone back into the ground. The hike proved interesting and exhilarating.

After working up an appetite hiking, Dustin started supper. I led the horses to a nearby stream to drink then fed them a container of grain cubes. Supper was steak, roasted potatoes, peas and carrots. We giggled and laughed while making "smores" over the coals, for dessert.

We stored the remaining food in a bear resistant container chained to trees, left there by the warden service for just that purpose. The night was peaceful if you call being serenaded by wolves howling in the distance, peaceful. I snuggled close to Dustin.

****

There was frost on the ground when I awoke in the morning. I could smell breakfast cooking. Dustin yelled, "Come and get it, cowgirl."

He had scrambled eggs, biscuits, bacon, and coffee ready. I could get used to this treatment, I thought.

It was a chilly morning packing up. My fingers and toes kept getting cold and I had to warm them by the fire frequently.

"Boy, is it cold, or what?" I said between chattering teeth, as we rode side by side down the meadow.

"And that, my dear, is why we do not pack after August. It snows in the higher elevation anywhere from mid-August on and it's too dangerous to try to take guests over the passes."

"So what'll you do for the next few months?"

"I have a couple of weeks off to prepare for hunting trips. They are base camp and not progressive, and we do not go to the high peaks or over passes. Even then, we frequently encounter snow where we have to walk, not ride, the horses. It's not fun, but the hunters all know that this can happen."

"You don't hunt all winter, do you?"

"No, no, the law and the imposing amount of snowfall both prohibit it. I work at the Sleeping Giant Ski Area; you passed it on your left about four miles before my cabin. I used to supervise their ski school but now I work independently giving horse-drawn sleigh rides December through March. I still get to ski free. After that, I have about a three-month break and go back home to help out during foaling season. I also train a few of the youngsters before I begin packing again the last of June."

"I didn't know you skied too. I've skied downhill for the past fifteen years, on local mountains in Maine."

"I didn't know you skied either. Guess there's a lot we still don't know about each other. I'd like to find out more. I've never known a lady like you."

"You mean one who doesn't mind getting down and dirty in horse dust and manure?"

"Yeah, that and other things. How about coming to work for me, with me, next summer? I really like you."

"I *really* like you too, but next summer is a long time from now and I live *many* miles away."

They rode for a while in silence, then Dustin said, "How many miles between Wyoming and Maine?"

"About 2500 too many," I replied with a touch of sadness.

EPILOGUE

Rimrock Ranch is still a dude ranch in Wapiti Valley, Wyoming. Gary and Dede Fales (Glenn and Alice's son and daughter-in-law) now own and operate it. They entertain up to 30 guests at the ranch during the summer months and schedule snowmobile trips for guests into Yellowstone National Park in the winter. In addition, they have a swimming pool outside the main lodge.

Sadly, Glenn Fales passed away, but Alice still lives in Cody and helps at the ranch whenever she is needed.

I returned to Maine to operate my own roller skating business through the fall, winter, and into spring. I went back to work at Rimrock Ranch as a ranch wrangler and guide for the next two summers. I was their head wrangler my second summer.

Razan (Raisin) never returned to Wyoming. On his trip back to Maine, he suffered severe scrapes, his right hip was bare to the bone, and other cuts and bruises from a loose petition in the horse van. He recovered with no permanent lameness albeit some scar tissue. He is still handsome, strong, healthy, and ridden on trails regularly.

The Wild Horse Race, although exciting, is no longer featured at the Cody Stampede. It was deemed inhumane treatment to animals.

One of Wyoming's favorite country music singers Chris LeDoux succumbed to cancer and died July 2005.

The boys, (Petre, Rand, Sean, Cole, and Travis) all returned to Rimrock working as mountain or ranch wranglers for the next two years. Petre received his college degree in Veterinary Medicine in Italy. Rand is a patrol supervisor with the Gallatin, Montana Sheriff's Office. Sean is a special agent with the Idaho Falls Fish and Wildlife Services. Cole runs his own outfitter's business packing into the Shoshone National Forest and Teton Wilderness. I lost track of Travis, but the last I heard, he still lived around Cody.

Dustin continued to run his own packing outfit into Yellowstone Park and the Teton Wilderness for the next two years then moved to Montana. His parents retired and, literally, passed the reins to him to run their mustang and Quarter-horse breeding ranch.

Printed in the United States
78271LV00002B/1-99